The Silence of Frogs

The Silence of Frogs

THOMAS TIMMINS

ISBN 979-8-9927154-1-5
Printed in the United States

Library of Congress Cataloging in Publication Data has been applied for.
Subjects: Fiction, Speculative Fiction, Environmental Fiction.

Published by Zoëtown Media

ZOË TOWN ®

A registered trademark
of Zoëtown Media Greenfield, MA

www.thomastimmins.com

Cover art and illustrations by Thomas Dudley
sightlab.com

Cover design by Tugboat Consulting
tugboatconsulting.co

Book design by Maureen Moore
The Booksmyth

Dedication

To all unsung women
dreamers, thinkers, writers, scientists

For a creative, caring, beautiful future
for all of us and our descendants

CONTENTS

"I love frogs! Especially the little ones
I can hold. I put one on my shoulder
and it just sat there."

Billie Beatrice Timmins

She sits and sits, like a clod of grass, her eyeballs
fixed and glassy, the slim tongue uncurls, curls
in her mouth: although she cannot fly
she eats what does. And then,
staring down into her losses, into the pool
that swaddled her among her mute companions,
Frog fills her throat with air and sings.

Ellen Bryant Voight

Brékkek Kékkek Kékkek Kékkek!
Kóax Kóax Kóax!
Ualu Ualu Ualu! Quaouauh!"

Frog chorus night song
Finnegan's Wake, James Joyce

BOOK I

THE SILENCE

A Silent Revolution

Not a peep

Not one frog croaked, thrummed, chirped, quacked, or trilled. Not one ribbit was heard. Not a gack. Not a gung. Not a cluck. Not a twang. Not a peep.

No bullfrogs demanding female attention, not one deafening frog rock concert. No soothing tree frog lullabies in the evening.

The wood frogs' screeches ceased. Not a yap or yowl from barking tree frogs. Where were the tiny peepers whose tinkling cries charmed everyone? The boreal chorus frogs stilled their calming chants. No pig frogs' grunts.

No proud male bullfrogs droned over and over "I'm the one. I'm the one." No females whispered their high pitched "Maybe. Maybe. Maybe."

The only sounds emerging from the ponds came from an occasional scratchy cicada call or cricket chirp. Hermit thrush rills arose now and then like tiny church bells. Crows squabbled off and on. In the night woods, barred owls invited prey to take a chance and whippoorwills' forlorn melodies amplified the surrounding silence.

Near a small town, across the river in a sprawling

swamp, the vast community of frogs thrived. They were cultivated by the world's largest frog farm for French, Thai, Cajun, and Filipino chefs around the world.

One of the unique features of Frog Frolic Farm was that, on any given day, the number of frogs that burrowed into the silt and mud to nod off or die equaled the number of frogs that woke up or matured from tadpoles. The pitch and volume of frog calls remained steady throughout all four seasons.

For years, the frog choir had delighted the romantics and comforted even the most melancholic of the townspeople.

When the background music of their lives disappeared, the daily world became a puzzling place. Many elders wondered what was wrong with their hearing.

Sightings of buzzards patrolling were normal, especially in the warm evening currents rising from the ponds. Now it seemed a wide, greasy kettle of vultures invaded the sky. Everybody feared the frogs were diseased or had died and the female frogs would never spawn.

The Farm's day supervisor said, "Remember when the kid let his pet alligator loose in Blue Boy pond? He ate half the frogs before we captured it."

The farmers inspected every inch of the ponds and their shores. No hidden alligators.

Was it the weather? Couldn't be. The Farm was amphibian heaven – breezy and coolish much of the year, plenty of sun.

Was it the frogs' reaction to increased nighttime temperatures of the water and the muck?

What about noises? Frogs fall silent if they hear an unfamiliar or loud sound. They go quiet if they feel the earth under their toe pads vibrating too much.

Had high school kids been partying out by the Farm?

Had the number of trains rumbling past the other side of town increased?

Did exhaust spewing from old farm trucks' tail pipes accumulate in the frogs?

On close scrutiny, the farmers of Frog Frolic Farm could find nothing wrong with the frogs. No sign of the dread fungal disease chytridiomycosis. No sign of weak muscles. No sign of scale. No sign of cloudy eyes. No split webs or cracked toes. The tadpoles wiggled and slithered in tiny schools.

Adult frogs peeked out of the water, their tongues darting at snacks in the air. They sat or burrowed like they were supposed to. Or they hopped, dived, rippled the water as usual.

But the frogs' only sounds were faint splashes when they leapt into the water.

Harold, one of the oldest farmers approached James, the Frog Frolic owner. "Remember that lightning strike in Amber Pond when you were a tadpole yourself? Your dad and us lost every frog and water snake and fish and all those ducklings nesting on the edge. The lightning evaporated the water and baked the ponds to cracked mud."

"I don't remember the strike itself," James said. "But I know we had one."

"Yeah, it took a few weeks to fill the ponds. The frogs didn't come back all the way for months."

"I heard that," James said. "My dad said we almost lost the farm. Now, since we have lightning rods everywhere, I think the ponds are okay."

"What I mean is," the farmer said, "could that have anything to do with the silent ones now?"

"Yeah, maybe. Some of the frogs back then could have had their DNA damaged," James said.

"Whatever happened, we're stuck with it."

"Right, Harold," James said. "We'll check everything we can."

Ever optimistic, Harold said, “Back in your dad’s day, we had a drought so bad the barn burned down. You remember those floods when the wetlands turned into lakes? That was when you were still a tad.”

James smiled and nodded.

“We had to build the sluices higher to stop the flow from washing away the ponds. We adjusted,” Harold said. “Never missed a shipment. We can do this. People eat the meat, not the croaks.”

The frog farmers dug random holes in the pond sludge seeking frogs and frog remains to analyze. They found some bloated frogs lying on their backs on the shores, their tongues hanging out in exhaustion. Buried frogs were hard to find. They decompose quickly, their bodies dissolving into mud and water.

The desperate Frog Frolic staff tried everything to revive the frogs’ voices. The farmers stirred the pond muck to wake resting frogs from their naps. The few frogs who opened their eyes chirped and croaked in bewilderment, then fell back to sleep.

The farmers, who usually wore ear protection because frogs at their randiest could shriek louder than rock guitars, now spoke in hushed tones and stepped lightly as they worked.

They established a quiet zone around the ponds, posting signs.

No Vehicles Allowed
Not Even Bikes

They upgraded the security cameras overlooking the

ponds hoping to capture images of intruders.

The farmers sprinkled sluggish flies on the water, drizzled lily pads with iridescent green bugs, refreshed the water flowing through the ponds, doubled the frogs' daily ration of fingerlings and day old salamanders and newts. The frogs ate everything but made not a burp or a peep.

The farmers researched 'silent frogs' and 'loss of frog croaking' and 'frog vocal paralysis.' They found nothing about frogs going quiet when they should be crying out for their mates.

The hush of frog calls became known on the farm, then around town, by the ominous name "The Silence." In the humid and lush world of the Frog Frolic Farm, a silent revolution began.

The LFA

The colony of frogs inhabiting Frog Frolic Farm's five ponds shared the swamp with abundant animal life.

The ponds originated in the wetlands upstream from "Slow Brook" and were connected by short streams with sluices.

"Cow Lily" was the pond where the yellow lotus-like flowers flourished and "Cattail" for the pond whose shores were dominated by six-foot tall cattails. "Blue Boy" bore blue-green algae, while "Goldilocks" produced brassy algae next to the smallest pond, "Amber," named for its ever-shifting collage of red and brown algae.

The soggy ecotone between the wetlands and the woods, was the region called "The Remotes." Its abundant wildlife, including feral frogs, fed predators as they made their way toward the ponds.

During countless generations, the frogs had evolved to avoid most predators' beaks and claws and mouths while keeping the Farm resonant with their melodies.

A few decades earlier when James was a teenager, his

father's breeding techniques caused a mutation that allowed the male and female frogs of every species to sing, croak, chirp, and mate throughout the year.

Or so the theory of went. James admitted nobody really knew why or how the mating calls of frogs pealed year-round. Whether due to mutation, breeding, or something else, the frogs coordinated their natural year-long rhythms. Being born, feeding, growing, dodging carnivores, calling, hopping, swimming, meeting, mating, laying eggs, hibernating, and being harvested – all in dependable harmony.

This coordination of nonstop frog reproducing and reaping made Frog Frolic the envy of the world's frog farmer tribe.

Years ago, when the townspeople living near the Farm realized the frogs had begun to call throughout the year, they raised their own cries to the town council and the county government objecting to the noise.

By then, it was too late – nonstop croaking and trilling and yapping and peeping had infected all the frogs. Eventually, the people adapted and soon stopped complaining. The Chamber of Commerce began promoting the hubbub of the frogs as a year-round symphony of Mother Nature.

Once the townspeople accepted and listened day after day to the amphibian soundscape, many began to feel a connection with the sonorous calls. They became attached to the bullfrogs' timpani and the treefrogs' xylophonic exuberance. While most people didn't admit to feeling emotionally connected to the cold-blooded bog dwellers,

Molly, a retired and enthusiastic psychologist, proposed that some people were more connected to frogs than others.

She claimed that, due to a person's Nature Intelligence, one of eight multiple intelligences, she and the others who felt a spiritual attachment to the frogs were extra-sensitive, tuned in to the natural world with high Nature IQs.

When the frogs stopped singing the Nature geniuses felt a loss almost akin to the death of a friend, while many in town enjoyed the sinuous silence.

Feelings of loss triggered an outburst of anger in the members of *Leave Frogs Alone, the local environmental group.*

Outraged LFA members protested the cruelty of breeding frogs for meat while ignoring their natural purpose of simply being part of the swamp world.

"It's the beginning of the end," they agreed. "Nobody can deny it now."

Following the lead of *Roots & Shoots*, Jane Goodall's worldwide environmental action group, the LFA expanded its recruiting.

"Frogs have been on earth for two hundred million years!" the LFA proclaimed. "Frogs have rights, like people. In the water, they're like canaries in coal mines. Leave them alone or we'll all pay."

LFA members and younger kids and even their parents grew up with frogs in home aquariums. As pets, the frogs thrived. Some lived for more than twenty years. The oldest pet frog was fifty-four.

"My grandma caught him when she was my age, six, almost seven," Rosa, already a budding scientist, told a local reporter about the town's oldest frog. "Henny was just a pollywog then. Gramma kept him in her bedroom.

"Henny was the only pollywog who didn't escape Gramma's room when it turned into a frog. The rest of them jumped all over the house and got away. Now Gramma's real old and Henny's still alive. I feed them flies and spiders. They like minnows and worms, too."

When asked if Henny was a boy or a girl, Rosa became thoughtful.

"Henny's African Clawed. Gramma named him Henry but then thought maybe he was a she. So, she called her Henrietta. We still don't know if he's a he or she's a she. That's why we call them Henny." Rosa said. "Henny's only three ounces, but they're one my best friends.

"Henny's skin is so soft. Sometimes it feels like silky fur. When Henny and I stare at each other, their sleepy eyes make me yawn. When I pick Henny up, I feel their little heart beat so fast it like when I held a hurt sparrow.

"People say frogs are grumpy. Not Henny. They smile at me."

Not only wild pond frogs stopped croaking and trilling, so did the pets in aquariums across town. When word got out the Farm had somehow caused the frog pets to fall silent, Rosa joined the LFA, its youngest member.

She said LFAers should go out to the ponds just to sit and listen. "Maybe they're whisper croaking," she said. "If we stay quiet and listen real hard, maybe we can hear them."

Every member of the club took several turns sitting and listening. They brought their phones to record any possible croak or chirp.

One of the dads supplied his high-fidelity digital recording microphones to the kids. They recorded two hundred hours of round-the-clock sounds, with samples from each Frog Frolic pond.

The recordings revealed soughs of wind in the cattails and shush of ripples against the shores, murmuring cypress leaves, duck quacks, bird whistles and calls. Cricket song and soft mutters between the listeners sounded pure and clear. The muffled engines of the farm equipment on their regular routes added daytime background chords. Occasional splashes from fish feeding at dusk and dawn and nighttime owl hoots and coyote cries and foxes barking rounded out the symphony emerging from the frogs' silence. During the day, thrushes and cardinals and all kinds of birds whistled their songs.

All night, whippoorwill whoops from deep in the forest comforted those who compared the birds' relentless three-note calls of longing to the continual calls of frogs seeking mates.

Haruki and Luis, who both aimed to work in the virtual reality field, edited the sounds into a half-hour song and posted it on the LFA website and its social media pages.

When the other kids and the adults in town listened, they felt awe at the pondside concert. As the farmers and some of the townspeople listened over and over, they became entranced by the variety of sounds soaring from the croaking- and trilling-free swamp.

Some heard a coordinated symphony, others heard jazz keyboards and woodwinds, some waited for solo outbursts, others heard a chorus of soprano, alto bass, and tenor voices. But no one heard the thump and beat of bullfrog croaks.

No barks, no burps, no groans.

LFA researchers discovered that green sea turtles worldwide were an endangered species. Herpetologists who specialized in turtles projected that most green turtles hatched in the coming decades would be females. Too few males meant far less reproduction and the ultimate loss of the species.

LFA members feared frogs might be disappearing too. They had to take action.

On the first Sundays of the month, the LFA marshaled protesters who marched at the front gate of the Farm holding signs and chanting.

The LFA glued photos of glamorous, multi-colored and patterned frogs on buildings and light poles all around town. Their website and social media posts relayed frog myths and stories and facts about frogs and their amphibian relatives.

They sponsored a frog video contest with the winners finding a place in the LFA Hall of Fame. The LFA asked for donations and funneled whatever they received to *www.savethefrogs.com*, a global center for frog preservation.

Next, the LFA sponsored a town-wide slogan contest: *Frogs sing the innocent soul of earth.*

Conversations among the members formed their own drumbeats of disaster.

"You used to hear them. Now you don't."

"Who's next?"

"It's scary quiet out there!"

"Frog song? Priceless!"

"Nobody wants to hear themselves think about The Silence."

"Everybody knows what they're telling us."

"Yeah. They're boycotting humans."

"We should do the same thing!"

Despite LFA's passion and dedication to the frogs, and the novel silence, Frog Frolic farmers and most townspeople dismissed the group as animal rights cranks, ignoring their objections as irrational.

Zasha, a non-LFA teen skeptic, pointed out the hypocrisy of the vegetarian and vegan LFA members by publishing his own Facebook pages and Instagram posts with images and videos of carnivorous bullfrogs "chowing down."

The famously predatory frogs were gorging on grasshoppers, worms, snails, and other bugs as well as dragonflies, moths, mice, smaller frogs, newts, snakes, and baby turtles.

"Just look at the facts," Zasha said on his YouTube video. "Everybody knows those frogs are pure predators. Nothing pretty about them."

On camera, he fed fingerlings, baby frogs, and chunks of hamburger to a bullfrog in his home aquarium.

"Where our good ol' American bullfrogs spread around the world, they annihilate native frogs, salamanders, all kinds of insect species. It's our job to keep 'em under control. Don't tell me frogs are cutesy little muppets!"

Five pounders

The year-round humidity coupled with average water temperatures of 60–70 degrees Fahrenheit and enough sunlight for leisurely basking was perfect for cultivating frogs. Morning mists in late fall and winter shielded the frogs from hungry predators. Evening mists in the rainy seasons charmed human visitors to the ponds.

As not only the largest frog farm, but as the worldwide leader in frog farming technology, Frog Frolic Farm sought to breed the plumpest *pelophylax esculentes*, the most common edible frogs. Wild full-grown females weighed in at a few ounces and had bodies only three inches long. James's father's first breeding goal was to produce male and female frogs with thighs at least twice as large as normal.

They tried to breed the endangered Goliath female frogs from Cameroon with the oversized male American Bullfrog. The Goliaths could grow to a foot long and seven pounds. They made only slight chirping noises because they have no vocal sacs.

Frog Frolic had no success with this crossbreeding

experiment, so they let the Goliaths roam the frog ponds until the last of them seemed to have disappeared.

The researchers went back to cross-breeding bullfrogs until one day they announced they'd developed five-pound male bullfrogs that had a melodic mating call and three-pound females who laid clutches of ten thousand eggs.

Once they accomplished frog giganticism, the farmers noticed that the big ones couldn't leap. They swam with powerful kicks, their legs opening and closing wide and slow, each kick driving them a leisurely yard across the pond. The farmers called the giants "Jumbos."

The first generations of Jumbos became choice meals for owls, hawks, and coyotes. Over time they learned to stay away from the pond shores and linger underwater and hide in the cattails and shore weeds.

The five-pounders tasted fine, though a little blander than the normals. Still, most customers preferred frogs in the one-pound range that would work best in their usual recipes.

Pragmatic commerce ruling their decisions, the Farm gathered up and sold the Jumbos to frog leather artists in Indonesia and Vietnam. The frog skin market was small, so they abandoned the breeding project.

Frog Frolic stored the five-pounder algorithms in the cyber-secure cloud and locked away stem cells in the lab.

Every so often a five-pounder showed up sunning itself on at the edge of a cattail coppice. Nobody bothered checking to see if they were crossbred Jumbos or original Goliaths.

Diva time

The American bullfrog was the world's most popular source of frog legs for food and skin for fabric and organ cells for medical research.

The loudest croaker, a bullfrog claiming his dominance, led the daily and nightly frog symphony. Among the throngs of songsters, each season of the year, one bullfrog's voice in each pond barked out above the others with power, timbre, and endurance.

Frog farmers whose ears were attuned to frogs' voices could tell a distress call from an after-dinner burp. Others declared they could tell which ponds rang out with the most urgent mating cries.

The first note the town's human babies heard was an E that sounded like an acoustic guitar string strum. Local musicians could distinguish the notes different species of frogs sang.

In the days before The Silence, on the three nights preceding the full moon every month, the frog ponds erupted in a frenzied racket, then fell almost quiet for a night or two.

The high school music teacher took the band for regular visits to the pond. She asked them to identify the different instruments the frogs used in their performances.

"Use your ears ... and your imaginations," she ordered. "Listen for the tempos – adagio, allegro. They're there. We don't know why. Sometimes you'll hear a tremendous crescendo followed by pianissimo, then maybe a Great Pause."

The first violinist, often someone dreaming of an orchestral career, might say, "Is it because the laws of music are natural laws, like math?

A budding rock drummer might chime in with beats from the drum section. "Could it be the frogs" *boom boom* "taught the humans" *boom boom* "how to compose" *boom boom boom* "symphonies!" *Boom boom boom.*

The classical students heard trombones, trumpets, violins, bass, flutes, a tuba, a piano, a triangle. The marching band identified snare drums, bass drums, and trumpets.

The local pop band insisted the bullfrogs were electric bass guitars and the tree frogs formed surround-sound lead guitars. The jazz players heard vibraphones and cymbals and alto sax flow off the ponds. Rappers built rhymes on beats and undertones from different sites on the ponds' shores.

Older frog farmers called some of the bullfrogs the Beethovens and the Korns and Radioheads. The night-trilling tree frogs became the Fluters. Younger frog farmers named their favorite loudest frogs for the rap musicians CleoII and FreeNite.

The church organist insisted she heard repeated

croaking and trilling that she was sure were the three notes opening her favorite Bach piano concerto. She claimed to know that many German classical composers based their low cymbal notes on the huffing sounds of moor frogs.

A Frog Frolic Farm legend maintained that female frogs dominated the ponds for a few random days every month, chirping, blurting, humming. People called them the Divas.

During Diva Time, in the thralls of frog romance, the possessive males became violent, protecting their territory from other suitors.

The protector and the invader wrestled, chest to chest, wrapping their forelegs around each other, paddling hard and pushing until one boosted the other over onto his back.

The loser hurried away while the winner proclaimed himself champion by an outburst of rapid croaking, declaring his temporary kingdom and his rights to any enticing ladies who might wander in.

For a few species, a male frog's calls invited a covey of silent females who tussled with each other for the rights to the male. The winner then floated off with the male to a safe, quiet place in the swamp.

Despite the mating hullaballoo and intensity, frog ferocity is combined with delicate sensitivity toward danger. When they hear a telling vibration from the land (fox? bobcat?) or in the water (duck? snake? big fish?), they fall silent in a Great Pause and sink into the mud, awaiting an All Clear signal of stillness and calm.

Anxiety

At Frog Frolic Farm, James had never ventured into genetic manipulation. Traditional breeding and cross-breeding techniques had resulted only in improved longevity and size, so the farmers questioned the notion some held that a rare mutation had silenced the frogs. But the frogs' sudden and universal end to their tunes bewildered the farmers and everyone in the area who was the least bit expert in the realms of froggery.

Frog sounds had chimed the notes of days and nights and seasons for decades. Now, having lost the soft leathery chords of their days and velvety tunes of their nights, many citizens felt disoriented in time and space.

Without the frogs' comforting daily and nightly melodies and rhythms, a miasma of gloom rose from the ponds, seeping into the neighborhoods near the Farm.

Accustomed to the rasps, croaks, chirps, even the faint tinkles, townspeople felt lost in The Silence. Without the slight but consistent vibrations in the air, their ears ached in the ominous hush.

With no steady rhythms of the background sounds,

some elders felt their hearts beating a little faster than normal and their blood pressures rising. Laid back retirees experienced the jitters. Some told of sweaty palms and shortened breaths. Some wondered what day it was.

While most people in town had long before The Silence stopped consciously hearing the constant frog calls. When they ceased, many admitted to sometimes feeling on edge, restless.

One woman said frog song somehow swathed her in safety. Without it, she said she felt exposed to danger.

At the coffee shop, even the grittiest of the crowd spoke of losing their mental anchors.

"I could feel the old frog calls. On my skin and somehow deep in my brain I felt a soft touch. Now I feel like I'm undressed or something. I'm a worrier but now I'm more worried."

Another commented, "It creeps me out."

Gossiping and storytelling and political discussions were normal conversational fare at the shop, but sharing vulnerabilities was new to the morning coffee crew.

As the revelations flowed, the former mayor said the skin on the backs of his hands felt raw. "Like The Silence ripped off bandages I didn't know I had."

Rosa's grandmother, Elena Maria, a devout woman who prayed to St. Ulphia, the patron saint of frogs, said, "When I can't hear frog song, I feel like it's a punishment for our sins."

At dinner one night, Elena Maria told Rosa, "Frogs sing holy songs. They're pets of the Holy Mother. She loves their humble songs from the mud. Not like those proud hawks and herons, those flying devils who prey on the weak."

Some of the townspeople looked for someone to blame.

"What's with the Farm?"

"Why don't they figure it out?"

"I always knew James could never fill his dad's boots."

"James is a good guy. He's got a master's degree in Ag."

"He should sue somebody!"

"Yeah!"

"He has to find out who caused it."

"That'll be the day."

"He'll figure it out."

"It came so sudden."

"Those new farmers they brought it from ... where was it .... Nigeria, Chile, like that? They screwed up everything."

Others expressed their sympathy for the Farm and farmers.

"Who else would process the frogs? Our local boys don't mind sloshing in the mud, but they quit working in the slaughterhouse years ago."

"The new people are solid. They learn English right away."

"Yeah, it's all about jobs. We need 'em."

"Frog meat is frog meat no matter if they croak or not."

One of the critics rejoined, "Yeah, croak. That's what I think about all the time now, frogs croaking, me croaking."

A murmur of uncomfortable chuckles and wistful smiles spread through the group.

A new therapist in town, trying to make connections, dropped in on the Coffee Club. Saturday was a good time to meet folks and let them know her availability. People from toddlers to retirees gathered, chatted, sipped coffee and smoothies, and welcomed newcomers to the town or just to the café.

The therapist listened to the range of viewpoints with interest. She didn't understand why so many people were distraught by the frogs' silence. She decided to add her professional opinion to the conversation to help move the people toward a happier place.

"You know," she ventured, "sometimes for the sake of our emotional health, we have to accept change and adapt. Make the best of it."

Some of the old timers at their table in the back stared at her. The former town roads crew manager, a curmudgeon with rigid opinions, shifted in his seat in a booth.

"No way people will accept this change to the town. Adapt? Ha. I'll be dead before this town adapts."

The therapist said, "I hear you, sir. I was wondering if you might consider this silence thing as a good. Something the town can use to heal its own shadow."

"The only shadow I care about is the one I sit in on my back yard Adirondack chair with a vodka tonic for company." He laughed and stood up. "I also like my own shadow as long as it's moving with me!"

A few snickers escaped from the group.

"Come on, old dunderhead. Sit down," the town clerk said.

Her husband added, "Everybody has a right to their opinion. Besides, she's new in town. It always takes newcomers a while to figure us out."

Frowning, the man sat down.

The therapist, embarrassed, didn't know how to respond without alienating the man and his friends. She said,

"Thanks for listening. I hope I can help somehow." She backed away toward the café's front door.

The curmudgeon waved, dismissing her, while his friends called, "Come on back any time."

"We can explain."

"He doesn't mean any harm."

The therapist nodded, threading her way past the customers, and left.

Some of the citizens expressed their fears by creating and cultivating conspiracy theories.

"It's the CIA testing drugs to understand how to keep us all quiet when they take over the country."

"No, that's the FBI. CIA wants to take over the world."

The conversation heated up.

"Yeah! Wipe out the first amendment."

"What's that?"

"Free speech. Duh!"

"It's a high tech thing. A satellite was laser beaming down and hit the ponds rather than it's tower."

"I heard it's the desert countries. China, Saudi Arabia. They want to suck the water out of the ponds, send it over like they do from Arizona."

"Yeah, then they'll come into and build high-priced condos on where the Farm used to be."

The more outrageous the theory, the more fun the townspeople had.

When the mayor heard some of the crazy notions, she said to her husband, "Babble is good. It keeps the people's minds off any of their real problems they can't fix."

The coffee shop was not the only place The Silence added

a sober tone to usual small talk. It seemed everyone in town had an opinion or a belief or a feeling The Silence invited them to share.

In the stands at school sports events, from the Ladies and Mens Auxiliary to the Volunteer Firefighters Association monthly meetings, after church or prayer services, during casual phone chats, and anywhere people hung out, someone always brought up The Silence.

A lobsterman from Maine who'd retired and moved to town to enjoy the year-round mild weather offered his new bridge club friends what he hoped was a consoling thought.

"You know, out on the water you learn silence is the natural state of things."

Gloria, the 87-year-old founder of the bridge club and an avid internet user said, "Don't be so sure about that. I like astronomy. There's a kind of sound inside outer space vacuum. Our instruments pick it up as static, but it's a sound."

"That could just be the technology," another piped up.

"You know about the *om* chant, right?" the leader of the yoga studio said.

A few of the bridge group raised their eyebrows.

"It's a Hindu thing," the yogi said. "When you chant it, you can feel the vibrations at the core of the universe."

The high school physics teacher, said, "Maybe that's the sound of the quanta bouncing off each other in the quantum flux."

Ignoring him, the other bridge players at the three card tables in Gloria's living room chimed in with their opinions about the universe and its sounds and silence.

"What about the music of the spheres?" a player asked.

"Isn't that an old Greek myth?" another replied.

"Well, whatever it is, it's damn quiet here. Who cares what happens on Mars or in the quantas and such?"

"That's right. Forget the silence. It's all around everywhere. I'm tired of it."

"Who needs it," the oldest member added. "I'm too close to the Forever Silence up at Angel's Rest cemetery."

"That's right."

"You said it, sister."

"Life is noise!"

"A lot of people need hearing aids is what I think," someone muttered.

"What?"

"What?"

Everybody laughed.

The yogi said, "Even if they do, it takes three months to get an appointment at the audiologist."

"My husband, he's what they call a 'selective listener' when it comes to me," the fire chief said.

"Silence is pure mind," the yogi said.

"Let's not fight, now," Gloria said, peacemaking. "We're here to compete, not squabble."

The weakest player in the club was antsy. "Let's be quiet and keep our minds on the game." Without looking up, he mumbled to himself, "I'm winning this hand."

At the end of their games, the players agreed the discussion added tang and a pleasant distraction from their usual tedious sessions where the most excitement came from a strong opening bid.

Gloria and the physics teacher both promised to dig into silence and report at their next monthly meeting.

Among other elders, without the frogs' nighttime chirps and chitters to lull them into dreamland, insomnia spread.

Adults of all ages wandered the town's Main Street as if sleepwalking, bumping into each other, forgetting why they were there.

After a drowsy driver nearly ran down a fog-headed jaywalker, the police chief declared a five mile per hour speed limit on Main Street.

Progressive religious leaders in town worked to come up with spiritual solutions based on their grasp of the Frog Way of life.

The rabbi urged her temple members to listen to more klezmer music, maybe even learn to play.

The mullah told the members of the mosque to listen and learn to sing together. Or, for those who wouldn't sing, maybe in this emergency, they could take up Sufi dancing.

Choirs at the Christian churches attracted new members. Organ lessons became popular. Kids in Sunday School drew and painted St. Ulphia.

Downloads of European, Indian, and Chinese classical music as well as African beats and Latin American salsa and flute sounds landed in the phones and computers of most adults.

The young listened to whatever music they always listened to.

Despite the spiritual and musical therapies, visits to the doctors in town quadrupled and the local pharmacy had a hard time keeping up with prescriptions for depression, sleep, and pain.

Once word of the therapist's offer to help people deal with the anxiety and depression rising from The Silence, her practice took off.

The police and the emergency room docs reported an increase in cases of opiod and heroin laced with fentanyl overdoses, but no deaths or real spikes.

When news of two suicides within a month traveled through neighborhood chatter, the medical community and the town health department held their breath.

Doctors began to worry, fearing black market incursion of depressants and euphorics. They asked their patients if they needed something different or if they'd begun to feel better.

"Doc, I'll try anything."

"We'll get by."

"Silence is Strong!"

A few months into The Silence, several high school students announced through all their social media, tweets, and texts "Silence is Strong!" Then they stopped speaking. They wrote their words or waved their hands in faux-American Sign. Some of them hummed their words or played beats on a random surface.

Parents tried everything from threatening the kids with grounding and stopping their allowances to taking away their phones and car keys. Anxious mothers took their kids to their pediatricians.

Thorough examinations of noses, mouths, throats, larynxes, lungs, and reflexes revealed no serious problems beyond routine swelling from allergies or colds. Some kids showed chronic irritation from their ear buds. A few registered minor hearing losses that caused squabbles between them and their parents.

Parents convened a meeting where they agreed to schedule visits to a variety of specialists, including psychologists. Blood samples sent to the university's teaching hospital lab came back normal. After examining the kids, every otolaryngologist, every sports doctor, every ophthalmologist declared almost all the silent young people healthy, except for the uncommon ear issues.

Lengthy questioning by therapists and even a psychiatrist, answered by written notes and hand signals and mimed emotions, resulted in prescriptions for anti-depressants and, in two cases, for anti-psychotics.

Unknown to the parents, the kids didn't take the prescriptions but hoarded them, especially the anti-psychotics. They'd heard the drugs might make for visions and high energy and good times, so they shared them with their friends.

The "mute" kids met in small groups under the trestle at the far end of the railroad yard. Talking and shouting and singing to each other, they exercised their tongues and lips. Their clandestine talk parties remained secret for as long as the kids' silence epidemic lasted.

The adult townsfolk began to wonder if the frog silence could be a disease contagious to humans. When the mayor came down with a sore throat and the rabbi developed a case of laryngitis, some parents scheduled appointments with their doctors and started wearing masks.

More and more high school students stopped speaking. Within weeks, most of the high school population went silent, gesturing and writing their responses and comments. Most high school classrooms fell completely silent since fear of contagion had spread across the town. Silence was the protection for the healthy, went a belief among the youth.

The senior class valedictorian, Jessica Chang, came to

school wearing a t-shirt printed with "In the Beginning was the Silence."

Before long, the slogan showed up on notebooks, in car windows, woven bracelets, on mugs and plates made in the school's pottery shop.

Several mothers, alarmed by the rising rate of kid silence and certain the silence was a rampant frog virus, insisted the town, maybe the state government, take measures to stop it.

Mask wearing became so common that mask refusers were shamed and even ostracized from clubs and sodalities. The coffee shop allowed only masked patrons to come in to pick up their coffees and snacks. The rebellious elders who met daily to sip coffee and share gossip met on the benches in the town park without masks.

Rosa asked her high school sophomore sister, "Carmela! Why don't you and your friends talk anymore? I want to talk with you right now!"

Carmela grinned, placing her finger over Rosa's mouth.

Rosa slapped her finger away, opening and closing her mouth, fluttering her lips. She squatted and croaked, hopping around her sister.

Carmela picked her up and hugged her.

"Whisper to me," Rosa said *sotto voce* into Carmela's ear. Carmela shook her head and hugged Rosa tighter.

Dozens of citizens volunteered to share their and their silent and speaking children's—DNA tests to help build a database for the researchers.

A current of dread coursed through the town, forcing the Frog Frolic Farm and the town council to ramp up their efforts to discover the source of the frog silence.

The mayor and the doctors marshalled a group of human and animal epidemiologists and signed up renowned psychologists from the state university to study the silence and solve the problem, if they could.

Confusion reigned.

"May the stars, may the flowers"

When the PhDs and MDs and other specialists descended on the town and set up interview stations in the schools and churches, the kids felt the town had been captured and occupied by a foreign army.

Word circulated that the Frog Frolic would expand its research into the frogs' silence to include scientists and amphibian scholars from around the world. The town's website listed the award-winning researchers it hoped to enlist for the work.

LFAers, now bored with their public silence and yearning for normalcy, decided they'd won and would return their voices to the town. The group selected kids who would break into whispering and muttering and mumbling, until their voices became clear. The rest of the high school followed over the next weeks. Once middle schoolers heard the older kids, they went back to their normal chatter.

Within days after the doctors arrived from out of town, before they had one interview, all the kids began speaking. As "mute" youth after youth spluttered back into speech, as if it were difficult, the adults congratulated themselves on their wisdom in bringing in the experts.

The LFA asked the town council for a meeting.

"We're talking and we have something to say to everybody."

The council agreed and LFA posted signs and social media announcements of the date and time.

The town hall meeting room overflowed with adults and bunches of swaggering high schoolers. The LFAers sat on the stage smiling and waving to the gathering.

When Cormac, a high school actor, explained *The Silence Strike* as a strategy to prod the adults to act, he apologized for any hurt it caused, giving a special nod to the town doctors present.

"We had to do it," he said. "You guys were pretending nothing changed. Now you get it – what are you gonna do about it?"

"You coulda talked to us like adults," someone shouted.

"Adults!" an LFAer shouted back. "You're the problem."

She glared at the crowd.

"You don't listen to our words, so we thought we'd see if you could listen to our silence. It worked."

Kids called "Yeah. We did it!" Fists pumped and bumped. *"We had a lot of fun."*

Cormac said. "All the world's our stage! Everybody can act. Right?"

He and the team applauded their peers for their Academy Award level acting jobs.

Cheers resounded from all the kids in the room. "L-F-A! L-F-A! L-F-A! L-F-A!"

At that, chaos erupted.

A group of adults ripped off their masks and started yelling. They rebuked the kids for how inconsiderate they were, how they scared the living daylights out of everybody, how they'd cost the taxpayers thousands of dollars.

One of the mothers cried, her voice rising above the bellowing, "How could you? I loved you and you did this to me!"

Carmela spoke up. "It was all of us."

Standing on her seat in the front row, Rosa called out, "Yay! Sister. Tell it!"

Rosa's mom, Lorena, still wearing her scrubs from her shift in the emergency room, shouted, "Carmela! Rosa! Go girls!"

Shrugging her shoulders, Rosa stared at her mother and mouthed, "Thanks, mom," then went back to chanting with the older kids.

The mayor tried to bring order to the meeting, but the humiliation and betrayal it seemed everyone in the room felt drove the noise level so high the windows vibrated.

Watching from the back of the room, the teachers who directed the school plays and monitored the Thespian Society stared at each other, afraid for a few moments that some of the parents would fly out of control.

As one, the LFAers and their classmates in the audience raised signs that said "SILENCE" and "SILENCIO." The adults ignored the signs, letting their disbelief and anger fuel more clamor and stamping.

The LFA and their friends shrugged and clapped their hands over their mouths.

When the townsfolks seemed satiated with their

bellowing and baying, the theater directors began to chuckle among themselves, sensing the deluge of would-be performers they'd soon have to work with.

The noise peaked, then fell as the adults read the signs, watched the kids, and began to understand. A few parents climbed onto the stage, hugged their kids, and smiling, shook hands with others.

At that point, the LFA leader shouted, "One more thing, folks. Read this!"

He waved a sheet of paper. When everyone looked at her, she said, "This is why we went silent."

The kids passed the handouts around. The leader waited until everyone had a copy, then read aloud.

> "May the stars carry your sadness away,
> may the flowers fill your heart with beauty,
> may hope forever wipe away your tears,
> and, above all, may silence make you strong."

The adults rustled the handouts, letting the message sink in.

"True."

"It's by a Native American chief."

"Cool."

Relief swept through the room as several of the angriest adults threw up their hands and started laughing. Tentative smiles rose on their maskless faces.

The LFA dropped their signs and circulated among the crowd, hugging and laughing. Younger kids scrambled onto the stage and jumped and hopped around, croaking and ribbiting. The meeting took on a festive air.

The LFA and the town council agreed the kids would speak and keep speaking as long as every effort was made to do more to bring back the frogs' voices.

The mayor thanked everyone and, frowning, said "At least we know we're all on the same page."

She revealed that none of the bloodwork showed anything unusual, other than high cholesterol for some adults and kids and, of course, the ear problems caused by the earbuds and the loud music.

Loud boos came from the kids.

The mayor grinned and urged people to get to back to normal. The next day the high school principal convened a whole school meeting in the gym.

Standing on the basketball court in front of the bleachers, she told the kids they'd done enormous damage to the town's identity and their parents' minds. Some of the girls and boys began to mumble and titter, withholding the heckles they were tempted to shout, while a few SILENCIO signs rose.

The principal raised her arms and shouted into her microphone.

"I love your spirit but ... but please, please don't do this again," she implored.

"Help the frogs!"

"Let 'em sing!"

A call and response chant rolled across the bleachers.

"Help the frogs!"

"Let 'em sing!"

"Help the frogs!"

"Let 'em sing!"

The principal and the staff waited until the hubbub died down.

“We’re doing our best,” she said. “We’re getting world class scientists on the case.”

Kids cheered, howled, punched the air, stomped their feet in a thunderous beat.

The principal raised her arms and shouted into her microphone.

“We’re done here, people. And ….” She waited until the kids quieted down. “Before we go … let’s make some real noise!”

The kids shrieked and screamed and roared. The gym rumbled and rocked and boomed.

Outside, the frogs stayed quiet.

Mr. Clemens

Investigations

Before the Silence Strike, the kids had taken research into their own hands. The Petco store at the mall three towns away became overwhelmed with orders for aquariums, swampy environments, mealworms, and crickets. Stage 2 and stage 3 Golden Food Nuggets were backordered for six months.

Red-eyed tree frogs were the most popular but some ordered horned frogs, blue poison dart frogs, and other exotic species. In the art classroom hand-painted and collaged frog care sheets papered the walls.

Rosa implored her mother. "Mommy, can I get a new frog? Henny needs company."

"Sorry, baby," her mother Lorena replied. "Maybe after Henny dies."

"No. Henny won't die. I need a new frog now. Henny wants a friend and I want a friend to stay with me all my life."

"Let's not talk about it right now."

Inspired by her mom's comment, Rosa said, "You're being a silent frog! Henny's lonely."

Lorena shook her head. “Let’s get Henny some fresh worms and bugs. I might have another idea, Rosamundo. Would you like to learn more about frogs?”

“That’s my favorite thing!” Rosa said.

Lorena smiled and hugged Rosa. “I’ll make it a surprise.”

“I can’t wait,” Rosa said. “Can you hurry up?”

Lorena didn’t know what the surprise would be, but something would come up.

“Patience, Rosa,” Loreena said. “When the time is right.”

“OK, mom,” Rosa said, disappointed.

During the Silence Strike, Frog Frolic’s frog veterinarian, Dr. Solberg, tested the water in all the ponds three times every day for excessive tetracycline, the antibiotic used to control harmful bacteria. All her samples measured normal.

With the help of the most experienced frog farmers and a dozen kids of all ages, Rosa included, she implemented a round-the-clock testing program. For days the anti-bacterial levels remained unchanged. She dropped the daily doses. Within two days, countless frogs fell ill, floating listless on the ponds. Hundreds died.

Dr. Solberg raised the level to the maximum recommended for frogs. In two days, she noticed vultures flying surveillance over the ponds. She and the farmers found parched but breathing and dead dried frogs lying on the shores. She reduced the tetracycline levels to normal and soon the torpid floaters disappeared leaving just a few idle vultures circling overhead.

Dr. Solberg expanded her research, fearing she could face a contagion far beyond her skills or equipment to detect. James and the farmers and townspeople held their breath.

Everyone at the Farm was relieved when, after examining hundreds of frogs, she once again confirmed the absence of the terrible *chytridiomycosis* fungus.

With no known cure for the frog silence, word came to James that no one from the state university Agriculture and Biology departments had any other research or treatment ideas except two: The silence was an undetectable invasion of a silence-dominant species that had spread a silence gene. The other possibility was an unperceived irritant that frightened all the frogs into silence, like constant sounds of predators approaching.

"Maybe. Still ...," James said. "Our tractors and pickups cruising around have never bothered them."

"A dumb idea," the farmers and citizens agreed. But they couldn't fully discard the notion.

At that point, Dr. Solberg, the farmers, and James held an emergency meeting. Frustration dominated the conversation. James realized that silent frogs would make his brand vulnerable to competitors, all of whom he considered run-of- the-mill frog farms. His "Singing Frog" brand was known worldwide for its tender and tasty meat and the luster of its hides.

Since most frogs remain silent except during their breeding seasons, many of the older farmers weren't worried by the quiet. "They're just going back to being frogs," they said. "The year-round breeding must have worn off."

Ashanti, one of the youngest farmers, with an edge to her voice, said, "The pendulum swung back. It's nature's way. Regression to the mean."

She urged James to move the entire colony to someplace

else where they could start over with a few reliable croaking and trilling species.

The farmers cheered at the notion until Dr. Solberg pointed out that frogs' well-being depended on their location.

"They're not translocatable," the vet said. "Many of our species breed in the same pond they were hatched in. Not only that, nobody knows how many millions of frogs we have.

"We'd probably lose most of them if we moved. You saw what happened with a little change in the antibiotic."

At that point, she pressed James to bring in the smartest frog epidemiologist he could find to investigate The Silence.

In hopes the frogs had a novel but curable infection causing amphibian laryngitis, James hired one of the world's foremost frog biologists, flying her in first class from France. The expert, Yvette Shinawatra, a seventh-generation descendant of a frog farming family in Thailand, agreed to keep the Farm's dilemma and her research confidential.

"Of course," she said. "No problem. By the way, call me Dr. Yvette."

Dr. Yvette's personal unspoken mission was to protect her family's farm in Thailand from silence. Her father insisted she learn if The Silence was infectious and if it was, to cure it. If she couldn't cure it, she was to discover or invent something to prevent it from spreading.

Her father had spent a fortune so she could become an ace frog scientist. Now this research was a once-in-a-lifetime opportunity to prove herself to her father and the entire frog meat industry. She could make her family the dominant frog farmers in Asia.

Rosa's mother visited Dr. Yvette soon after she arrived in

town. Lorena told Dr. Yvette about Rosamundo's fondness for frogs and her interests in learning more about them. She asked if Rosa could spend a little time with her to learn about scientific research.

Flattered and curious about the girl, Dr. Yvette said, "Of course. She's about the age I was when father started teaching me about the lives of the frogs."

When Rosa heard about her mom's surprise, her life changed. She became a scientist in her mind. After school on a couple of days every week, and Saturdays when Dr. Yvette invited her, she tagged along. When the vet tested the water, Rosa read the results. She peered through the microscope getting her first glimpses of cells and other minute wiggly creatures. She touched frog eggs.

In the lab, Rosa felt as happy as she'd ever been.

One day, Dr. Yvette said, "From now on, Rosamundo, just call me Doc." Then she offered Rosa a scalpel and a plump dead frog on a cutting board.

Rosa needed one answer before she accepted the scalpel. "Will I hurt its soul?"

"No. It's dead. Besides, frogs don't have souls."

"My gramma says they do. Henny has a soul, I'm positive."

"Maybe Henny does," Doc said. "This one's dead. Its soul flew away into swamp heaven." Doc smiled and caressed the frog carcass splayed on the board.

Satisfied, Rosa didn't hesitate. She slit the frog's belly and giggled. Doc praised her precise knife work. Rosa peeled back the skin and, with her small fingers, gently lifted out the frog's stomach and lungs.

"Go ahead, Rosamundo. Be careful but take out all the organs."

Rosa picked up a tweezers and pulled out kidneys and an intestine. When she grasped another organ with no idea what it might be, she tore it in apart.

"That's okay. You're doing quite well for your first time. We have plenty of frogs you can dissect."

Rosa continued exploring, even probing into the back of the frog's skull and sliding out the tiny brain. She laid all the parts on a transparent plastic plate.

"Nice job. Tidy and organized," Doc said. "Now watch me."

Rosa watched, fascinated and eager to dissect more frogs. She liked the feeling of the scalpel slicing through the thin but tough frog hide.

"Doc," she said, "you can call me Rosa. All my friends do."

When Rosa described her dissections to Aleema and Melissa, her best friends, the girls winced.

"Gross."

"Yuck."

"Does it stink? All that slime."

"It's creepy."

"No," Rosa said. "I love it."

Her friends looked at each other, grimacing. "You're crazy," Melissa said.

"I'd heave if I did that," Aleema said.

"No you wouldn't," Rosa said. "Come with me to the lab. It's clean. You get used to the formaldehyde smell." Rosa laughed. "No blood, really. It's cool."

Squealing and gasping in disbelief, her friends pretended to vomit. Rosa watched, unimpressed but smiling.

Aleema straightened up first. “OK,” she said.

“Right now?” Melissa asked.

“After school tomorrow,” Rosa said. “Don’t tell your parents till after.”

“O god, why not?”

“They’d try to stop us. They don’t know it but frog guts are beautiful.”

Dr. Yvette approved of the girls’ visit, but told them she didn’t have much time to spend with them. They could watch her, but she couldn’t supervise them with knives and tweezers.

Rosa was disappointed. “Please, Doc?”

“I’m sorry, Rosa. I have a lot of pressure on me.”

She stared into Rosa’s eyes. “You’re my good luck mascot,” she said. “‘*Mascotte*’ we say where I live in France. You can watch me at work but I can’t let all you girls handle scalpels.”

When the girls left the lab that day, her friends teased Rosa. “Mascoot. Toot toot. Dat’s goot.”

Rosa didn’t mind. She liked being Doc’s “Mascotte.” They all laughed as they strolled down Frog Frolic Lane away from the lab and past the processing building.

Dr. Yvette continued her quest, dissecting hundreds of muck-brown frogs, blue-spotted frogs, cow lily-yellow frogs, bog-green frogs, iridescent green frogs, even a few precious glass frogs.

She drove around the county to sleuth out any unusual environmental factors. She toured a gas-fueled power plant, a plastics packaging factory, and a medical waste disposal firm operating in the county, upstream from the Farm.

They became her chief suspects as sources of frog-muting pollution.

When he heard this, James nodded.

"Could be," he said. "They've all been here for decades, but maybe they've changed the way they do things."

The farmers asked her to test for poisons, too. "We've got a trustworthy industry," they said. "But who knows? One of our competitors might have dumped something into the water. Rat poison or cyanide. There's some weird people out there."

Since frogs drink through their skin, Dr. Yvette conducted multiple tests to determine the radiation and chemical levels in the ponds, soil, and water. She also examined the water in and around the vernal pools on the Farm and in town, small ponds where water didn't drain well and where eggs hatched and tadpoles grew.

After checking and double-checking and triple-checking her work, Dr. Yvette wrote her monthly report to the Farm, "The Frogress Report." In it she discussed the locally well-known fact that frogs hear with their tympanic membranes behind their eyes and maybe with undifferentiated organs in their heads.

The lungs of all the species were normal. She stated she found nothing wrong with any of their vocal sacs – their bubbles.

"The bubbles I tested are fine," she wrote. "Fulsome, firm, and flexible. Bubbles and bellies inflate and expand as normal."

"The tympanic membranes are sound, *pun intended*! They vibrate as they should."

"However," the report continued, "PFAS do float. I doubt they have anything to do with the frogs' silence. They are in water everywhere.

"While inspecting the vernal ponds, I found one with slightly abnormal traces of caffeine in the water, perhaps because it is downstream from a diner.

"Upon further investigation, I discovered a slightly abnormal amount of a steroidal hormone in that pond. I retested the water in all the vernal and harvest ponds without finding unacceptable levels of any harmful hormones.

"To be safe, I recommend discontinuing use of that one vernal pond as a feeding and growing site for tadpoles. I also recommend monthly vernal pond testing."

Rumors of the imported scientist's results leaked. When the high school's environmental activists heard, they insisted something was wrong with the water and maybe even the bugs and slugs and minnows that frogs eat. They demanded that the frog scientist examine the frog tissue samples for contamination by micro-particles of plastic.

An LFAer said, "Everybody knows when it rains, it rains tiny pieces plastic. It's in human mothers' milk and all our cells so it's in the frogs. Bits of plastic are probably jamming up their throats."

Backing up their claims, Rani, a sixteen-year old leader, quoted a report from the World Health Organization. She said, "And I quote the WHO online '... microplastics are ubiquitous and have been detected in fresh water, wastewater, food, air, bottled water, tap water, even human breast milk.' They even found plastics in adults' cells!"

The farmers and the LFA organized a volunteer team of sample gatherers who collected specimens of water, mud, and plants from even the most remote parts of the marshes and streams that fed the ponds. The tests concluded the ponds were free of radiation other than natural radon in the air and soil and showed no unusual amounts of harmful chemicals.

Dr. Yvette constructed dozens of models of frog symptoms, comparing them to the known illnesses or misshapen anatomies of amphibians.

With her personal veterinary bot, Vetknow, Dr. Yvette scoured the internet for precedents and solutions. She consulted with veterinarians and wildlife biologists across the globe.

One new idea emerged: magnetic fields or microwaves interfering with frog larynxes. She tested all the ponds, the wetlands, and the air, finding no strange fields or waves.

Her resultant theory was that a gene change caused a structural mutation that was dependent entirely on the Frog Frolic Farm location.

Dr. Yvette presumed the cause of the silence could be inherited from a dominance of past genetic mutations. She asked James to collect samples of every species and age of frog they could find in the Farm's vernal pools and ponds.

The Farm sent living and dead frogs to the National Animal DNA lab. The lab's expensive scrutiny of the DNAs of the Farm's frog breeds indicated no mutational abnormalities, no patterns of brain or organ cell damage, other than the tendency of some frogs to grow large.

The lab compared their findings with past analyses of

the farm's frogs and other species. The conclusion: across the range of Frog Frolic species their current DNA profiles remained the same as they had been ever since the Farm had begun its random DNA testing years earlier.

In her final report, Dr. Yvette repeated that the frogs' throat pouches bulged as expected. The bubbles ballooned as if they were croaking. Their tympanic membranes were healthy.

All organs she examined were whole and appeared to function as she should. She attributed the frogs' health to an abundance of food, consistently fine amphibian weather, and the Farm's breeding and cultivation practices.

She added, "As to microplastics impurities, we found small quantities of plastic particles in many frog cells, less than three fibers per average whole frog, and less than six plastic fibers per liter of pond water.

This is consistent with microplastic contamination in this state. Thus, amount of plastic is of no new scientific consequence or implication in the loss of frog voices."

"As you know, certain long-lasting chemicals linger in the environment. They may or may not be responsible for frog silence.

"I recommend regular testing. If anything changes from today's baseline, that may give you a clue.

"I may be wrong, but it seems your healthy frogs live in and drink as clean a wild water as anywhere on the earth. We have to wait until our technology is advanced enough to analyze frog song atoms."

Dr. Yvette went home to France somewhat comforted since air and water pollution, microplastics, and random contamination from rival frog farmers were not new threats anywhere, even in Thailand around her family's frog farm.

To the town council, the mayor noted, "Microparticles of plastics are everywhere. We know that. It's depressing, but what can we do?"

At the urging of the mayor, James published Dr. Yvette's report. When the news flew around town, the high school kids protested for days around the Farm. They now had concrete evidence of plastics invasion everywhere.

The LFA didn't give up. They posted warning signs outside the town's water wells and at the entrance to Frog Frolic. They informed their peers and parents the U.S. had a falling birth rate "... due to the plastics affecting female hormones." Their theory was that plastics "or something in the water" had caused male frogs to fall silent. They speculated that the next thing that happened would be frog infertility.

Rosa, Aleema, and Melissa organized a session for their class about plastics and how to recycle them. The class then drew up signs and marched around the front of the school, chanting the LFA rallying cries.

"Leave frogs alone!"

"Silence is strong."

"Let the froggies sing!"

High schoolers in shop class welded scrap metal plates into casket-sized boxes for the activists to inter in a grave on the edge of the school campus.

The art class found a boulder in the woods, rolled it to the campus, and engraved the headstone.

Plastics hide in frogs, you, and me.
What do we do to be plastics free?

The students collected, shredded, and buried in the coffins their fleece jackets, childhood toys, water bottles, and all the packaging they could find.

Then kids of all ages, including the old folks in the assisted living residence, lobbied the town council to abolish plastic bags from stores. It did, immediately.

Toney, a natural comedian, offered a prize to the fellow student who could prove she or he had the most microplastic in their cells – the "Human of the Future" award.

He persuaded an internet DNA testing outfit to offer a discount to the students. Even the wealthiest parents, fearful of the results, refused to fund the "nonsense."

Ranidae rustlers

Frog Frolic frogs were raised in a habitat as close to wild as possible. Unlike conventional farmed frogs, none of Frog Frolic's frogs ever tested high for pesticides or herbicides in their fat. Its frog abattoir practices led the world in its humane treatment of 'frog stock' and had earned the highest safety and sanitation ratings from the municipal and state health inspectors.

Despite the plastic content of their frogs, everyone at Frog Frolic felt relief at the normal plastic counts. The Farm had marketed the frogs and their frog eggs as "all natural" and "organic as can be."

James employed a staff of hands to scare off the egrets and herons and wood ducks, the bane of the frogs and the farmers. They also eradicated nests of garter snakes and green vipers and other sneaky reptiles who could eat a morning's harvest of frogs in a night. Foxes and coyotes nosed around the ponds, but their dining habits didn't reduce the frog populations enough to bother the Farm's business.

Dr. Yvette's parting advice to the town had been that more townspeople should cultivate tadpoles in pure water. They could buy eggs from Thailand or Vietnam, where the frogs still croaked and sang, and raise them for Frog Frolic. She offered to arrange a shipment from Thailand of pollywogs guaranteed to grow up into full-throated peepers and croakers.

Some elders leapt at the idea and mobilized, forming a Pure Water Vernal Pooler club.

The high school Latin teacher, Mr. Emmet, a known wit and club leader, said, "Let's call ourselves 'The Rainy Day People.' *Ranidae* is Latin for the frog family, you know. We'll filter plastic from our vernal pools and raise pure hormone-free singing frogs."

Jokesters at the coffee shop called the vernal poolers "The Rainy Dazies."

The Silence was only the latest crisis James had dealt with. One of the first calamities James had faced when he took over the Farm was as bonkers as the "Rainy Dazies" years later.

One blazing September, long before the frogs lost their voices and just after James had expanded his colonies of frogs into five ponds, production fell dramatically.

James called in Sam Brody, a retired frog farmer to help. Sam had been in charge of egg harvesting and shipping. He considered himself a frog engineer and felt deep affection for the frogs. His strategy was to observe the frogs non-stop all day and all night, just in case he could spot anything unexpected.

Sam's plan worked. One moonless night, he saw some

long shadows slinking toward the water. He watched them swipe nets through the ponds, hoist their wriggling frog booty, and stuff them into bags they carried, then steal back through the woods.

James interrupted the sheriff's breakfast the next morning.

"We know what it is, Leon," he said. "Rustlers."

Leon started to laugh, gagging on his sausage. "No way," he said. "Rustlers?"

That evening the sheriff deputized the farmers, allowing them to bring their shotguns. A few non-deputized citizens showed up to get in on the action.

"Your guns are only for show," he said. "Don't fire them whatever you do."

No frog poachers showed up that night. Still, the sheriff and his deputies persevered.

Two nights later, at two a.m., four skulking frog rustlers found themselves surrounded by fierce frog farmers. The thieves ran for the trees. One of the thieves got tangled in cypress roots and another couldn't extract his leg from deep mud.

One of the excited frog vigilantes fired two shots into the air from his double barrel 12-gauge shotgun.

The rustlers shouted, "We give up."

"Don't shoot," the smallest begged.

"Wer' innocent. Jes' diggin' up some Indian taters and wild carrots for supper," another claimed.

With menace in his voice, the sheriff said, "In the middle of the night? Toss them nets and bags over here."

The rustlers let the plastic bags fall.

"Back away and keep yer hands up! Ovie, get the bags."

Ovie sloshed through the ankle deep bog and picked up the bags.

"Bring 'em here. Let's see what's inside."

Ovie brought the bags to the sheriff and opened them up.

"They're fulla frogs, sheriff."

The sheriff motioned to his deputies with guns. "Let's take 'em in, fellas. The farm's gonna be happy. Probably throw a frog leg cookout for you boys."

The posse laughed.

After questioning his prisoners, the sheriff unraveled the entire organization and soon arrested a gang of nine, all of them from out of town. He learned who their customers were and where the frogs would be shipped – across state lines – so he called in the FBI.

The FBI tracked down the distributors and their

customers who were selling not only across state lines but illegally exporting them to Europe and Asia.

The Frog Frolic Frog Farm made the global media, foreshadowing the later media circus when the frogs fell silent. Circulating the internet for a few days of humor, headlines read –

"FBI Called In. Frog Rustlers Corralled."

"Froggy Rustlers Muck Around – Get Swamped by Vigilantes."

"Criminal Charges Filed Against Brazen Frog Theft Ring."

Wags drew cartoons of ten-gallon hatted rustlers roping frogs amidst wild leaping and splashing.

While many townspeople thought Frog Frolic Farm was no more appealing than an ant farm or even a dairy farm, the Chamber of Commerce used the Frog Rustlers story to promote Frog Frolic Farm in hopes it would bring tourists to town and even new tax-paying residents to work at the Farm.

Mr. Clemens

Mr. Clemens, the Biology teacher who frog-farmed part-time to supplement his low teacher's pay, was the most popular teacher in the high school.

He had an endless array of frog stories, gross (frog pee and excrement), hilarious (frog conversations in which he'd play the roles of the chirpers and trillers), and just crude enough to keep the attention of the teenage mind.

In the first class of the year, he announced, "You think you're in Biology, some smelly subject about animals and frogs. With a lot of memorizing.

"You're partly right. The class name is Biology. It's about animals and everything alive. There are some smells involved. And they're not all fragrant."

The students giggled, wondering where this scrawny, balding, unshaven teacher would lead them.

"Biology is the most complex subject in the world – besides the person sitting in your seat right now."

Mr. Clemens grinned while some of the students nodded and others shrugged.

"Math, physics, chemistry – they're cool. But, to me they're as good as dead. All they can do is describe things, tell it like it is, nothing more. Like 2+2=4 or E=MC squared or hydrogen is the lightest element. It always will be."

Kids yawned, frowned, tapped their feet, having little grasp of where their teacher was going."

"But Biology ... biology is alive. Everything is changing, growing, dying, evolving."

Mr. Clemens pointed behind him to an ivy plant, the fish in the aquarium, the poster of bird life in North America.

"Let's start with a definition. Bio – life, logy – studies. You're in Life Studies. If you learn one thing here, it's that life is the only study." He paused. All eyes on him, he continued, "As long as you're alive, anyway."

The class sighed. His jokes were lame.

"The more seriously you take this class, the more fun you'll have. Ask anybody.

"We're going to study the entire animal kingdom. Our section on frogs, salamanders, toads – they're all a subsection of biology called Zoology – the study of animals. Here's the key to why we study Zo, and don't forget it – we're all animals!"

He stared at the barking boys until quiet returned.

"Yes, even if humans have really big brains and the power to think about the future, and we walk on two legs, some of us are more animalistic than others."

Subdued barks and growls and some meows and howls and grunts flowed around the room.

Ignoring the noises, Mr. Clemens went on. "We're in a bio-sphere – a globe of air and earth where things live," he continued, spreading his arms in a great circle. "Yes, dogs and cats and coyotes and pigs. And trees and mushrooms and bacteria and viruses and mosquitoes. All life that's always changing. Evolving."

"How about rain?" a kid asked.

"How about wind? It's always changing," said another.

"Good questions, but not rain. Not wind. Though they have living material inside them," Mr. Clemens said. He sensed he was starting to lose half the class. "Ok," he said. "Let's move on to the fun stuff."

Mr. Clemens' dedication to the worlds of animals and birds and frogs impressed the students. He was a demanding teacher and a tough grader. Still, every student, even those who didn't like science, took Mr. Clemens' Biology class.

The section on frogs and amphibians with stories and jokes and a lab was the highlight of the year. Mr. Clemens' enthusiasm rubbed off on the whole class.

Budding biologists edited and expanded Wikipedia pages. Inspired by the section on amphibians, and their studies of Mr. Clemens' recommended websites, *www.amphibiaweb.org* and *www.myfroggycam.com*, several students became fervent environmentalists, determined to reverse the global decline of amphibians and all other animals.

Students sorted themselves into 'squads' named for different species of frogs. The Rio Grande Tree Frogs competed with the Mink Frogs and the Pickerel Frogs for the best grades or prettiest paintings or most informative essays. The Garden Club kids started the Western Tomato Frogs and the Green Banana Frogs. Members of the school chorus and band chose names like the Kenyan Belling Frogs and the Haitian Drumming Frogs. Year after year, the Taiko Tads maintained their infamous reputation for booming thumps and beats.

The youngest boys showing off in class wanted to join the Blue Poison Dart Frogs or the Strawberry Poison Frogs but Mr. Clemens forbade petty mischief possibly leading to lethal mischief.

"No poison squads allowed. And no fake names like 'Bully Frogs' or 'Missile Tongue Frogs.' Yeah, I've heard 'em all .... You have thousands of species to learn about. Get hoppin'!"

When loud croaks boomed out or shrill peeps erupted in the classroom any time during a class, he would smile.

"Mimicry. Genetic predisposition. Random changes," he would say. "That's how we learn about our world and how it works."

He took the occasion to point to a collection of framed lists hanging on the wall. "Record your Frog Love Songs and symphonies. The coolest frog love song each semester and the best symphony will win the Golden Bubble award and have your name go down in infamy on the lists. I'll be the judge."

At that point, the kids groaned and started plotting their entries and their frog music squads.

In the first amphibian class of the year, Mr. Clemens said, "Let's bust a myth. Stand up if you think frogs are stupid."

Kids looked around. Nobody stood.

"That's right. Just like you, frogs are not stupid! Like you, they're also good-natured when they have to do what they have to do. Even their homework."

Mr. Clemens grinned when the class groaned, as they were supposed to.

"You know the old story? Put a frog in a pot of boiling water and it'll try to jump out? But put it in a pot of cool water, bring it to a boil – the frog will just keep paddling until it's cooked to death?"

The students knew the story.

"No way. False." Mr. Clemens shouted. "Frogs are smart!"

"Frogs are smart," the students whooped and barked in response.

"Put a bullfrog in a pail of boiling water, it will ....," he said, crooking his finger, inviting the answer.

Some class members smirked.

"Croak."

"Yeah, croak."

"Die."

"Expire."

"Give up the ghost."

"Ascend to frog heaven."

"Pass away."

Tossing his chalk up and down, Mr. Clemens said, "And, what else?"

"I know, I know," a polite girl would volunteer. "Kick the bucket!"

The class laughed and cheered.

"Nope," Mr. Clemens laid the chalk on his desk and went on. "Frogs are like scientists. They observe and evaluate everything. Just because the water is cool and warming up slow doesn't mean the frog will let herself boil and bubble, get in trouble."

Some boys would always holler, "Go, frog!"

"Put a frog in cool water, it paddles around, assessing its surroundings. If the water gets too warm for comfort, the frog jumps out. You would, so why not a frog?"

Kids would grin and exclaim, "If not me, why not a frog?"

A class clown would bark, "Why not a dog?"

His buddies would grunt and oink, "Why not a hog?"

Everybody loved Biology and Mr. Clemens.

When class calmed down, he said, "You know what else?" Mouths dropped open. Eyes widened. Grins up and down every row.

"You could call frogs a lot of things. Stupid. Gross. Slimy.

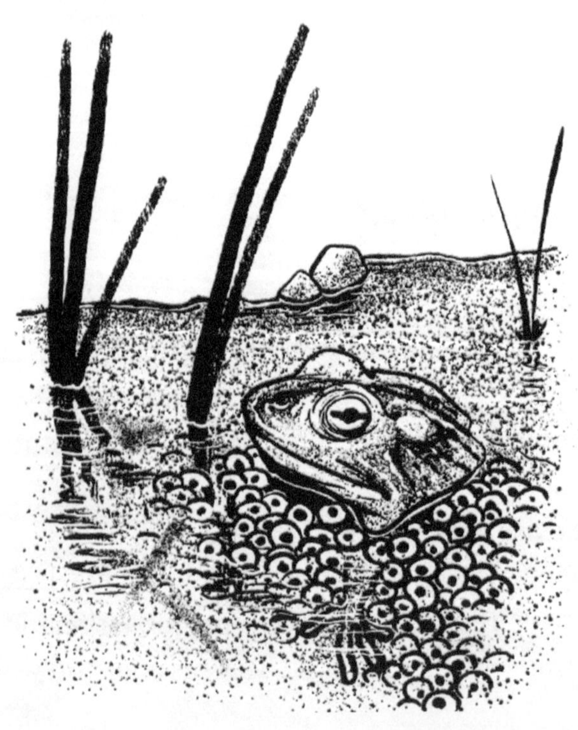

Hey, Frog Frolic Farm calls them a profit center. You know what I call them? Give me some words!"

The students shouted while Mr. Clemens copied the words onto the whiteboard.

"Smart. Slimy. Cool. Dissectible. Singers. Loud. Jobs." He raised his marker and waited.

Rosa, known as the frog expert in the group, "One thing you didn't say, Mr. Clemens."

She paused, he nodded and smiled.

"Frogs are miracles," she said. "Miracles of evolution. They transmogrifiy."

The kids looked at each other, expecting a Mr. Clemens joke. Since phones were forbidden in class, none of them could look up the word. Most students shrugged and waited for the punchline, except for some girls who said, "Tell us, Rosa! You know, girl!"

A quiet and conscientious girl, editor of the school newspaper when she wasn't working on a science project, Rosa smiled at her friends and shrugged.

Mr. Clemens nodded and everyone turned toward her, unsurprised. "Definition, please."

"Metamorphosis is the right word. Transmogrify means a strange change. Something crazy. Change like magic into something else. Like a frog to a prince." Rosa said. "Metamorphosis is a transformation from one state to another."

"Correct," Mr. Clemens said. "You all should know all three words."

"I know," Toney said. "Like my family moved from Maine to here. We transmogrified!"

"Yeah. Go, Toney!"

"Clever." Mr. Clemens smiled. "But no, not like changing your location."

"You're the crazy one, Toney," one of his friends shouted.

"What about trans people?" Pippin asked.

"I know, I know!" cried Benjamin, the son of the pastor of the Church of the Resurrection. "Like Jesus rising from the dead and turning into a spirit!"

The kids went silent for a moment, staring at Benjamin, then started drumming on their desks. Benjamin beamed.

Mr. Clemens waited, tossing his chalk up and catching it. When the class didn't pay him any attention, he picked up two more pieces of chalk and began juggling.

Eventually, the class calmed down, watching him.

"Nice, Mr. Clemens." A few whistles broke out then everyone clapped.

Mr. Clemens set the chalk down and perched on the edge of his desk.

"Ok, listen up. Trans kids is close. And, yes, Jesus did more than transform. He transmogrified."

A cacophony of whoops rang out! Benjamin raised his arms in triumph yelling "Yo! Jesus!" His crew stood up, raising their arms and eyes to heaven and echoed his triumphant shout.

"Pipe down, you guys!" Mr. Clemens said. "The class assignment is to write a five-hundred-word essay on transformation and metamorphosis in nature. All you have to do is look around. Think about grapes. They can transform into wine. Do they metamorphose?"

Kids raised their thumbs, toasting their teacher who let

them get away with so much in class. Sipping and slurping noises flowed from desk to desk.

“For your information,” Mr. Clemens went on, raising a finger to accent his point. “The part of Jesus as a spirit is not nature. That’s ‘transcendent.’ Think about one cell becoming two before it became trillions that make up you.”

The class buzzed.

“Think about fish crawling up the beach and learning to breathe and walk and fly. Think about the Lazarus wood frog in the arctic that lets the liquid between its cells freeze in the winter while the frog’s heart and lungs stop moving until spring.”

“We’re thinking,” Toney said. “It’s hard.”

Mr. Clemens grinned, focusing on Toney. “A philosopher said, thinking is so hard most people would rather die than do it.”

The class laughed. Another clown called out, “Don’t die, Toney.”

“Everybody, listen up. The more logical of you can see this as a problem to solve. Clemens said. “The more lyrical can use this as a chance to rhapsodize.”

“You mean like when you wrap a present?” Toney quipped.

Mr. Clemens ignored him, going on. “Use evidence to come up with a new idea. Crazy’s okay, as long as you make it yours. A theory, an intuition that leads to possible causes. I like a story. You can use your personal bots or any bot for suggestions or history.”

Several kids raised their hands. One of the boys, on a mission to be class leader in witty rebellion, shouted out, interrupting Mr. Clemens. "You mean we can use our Genies?"

"Of course," Mr. Clemens said, unruffled by the rude interruption. "Get together in groups, toss around your ideas."

"O. I mean, like, they'll tell us," Zahra said.

Ndeia spoke up. "Like, you know, my Roamer."

"Mine's Hooper," Samuel the basketball player offered.

"Bongo,'" Rod, the band's drummer, pounded his desk.

Destiny waved her hand, saying, "Mine's a knight. Mike Archangel,"

Honey stood up. "I have two. Moose and Mendel," she said. "After my dogs."

Mr. Clemens raised his chalk and swung it around like a symphony conductor. "All of them," he said. "In fact, mine is Franklin named after Ben and Rosalind."

When some of the kids' faces broke into puzzled frowns, he said, "Ask your genies about them."

They started poking into their pockets and bags to pull out their phones. Mr. Clemens clapped and said, "After class."

He waited for silence, then said, "Consult your genies but write your essays in your own voices. I'll know if it's you. I won't mark you down for a few misspellings or grammar mistakes. Franklin won't either."

"Essay due in one week." Mr. Clemens clapped his hands. "Class dismissed."

On the way out, kids mumbled and joked.

"I'm doing caterpillars and butterflies," Kai said.

"I'm doing cucumbers," Levi said.

"What? A cuke is a cuke," Gabe rebutted.

His friend poked him. "Sure it is ... until it's a pickle!"

"I'm gonna do potatoes – mashed, fried, hash browns!" Tavi shouted.

Will, the most conceited boy in the class, said, "I have some good ideas about how I transmogrified from nothing into me!"

Mr. Clemens overheard, saying, "Good idea, Will. If you do a good job, I'll let you read your paper to the class."

Will grinned and strutted while everyone else groaned.

Rosa had listened carefully to Mr. Clemens. The insights in the biology essay she wrote at fifteen explaining the hypothesis that transformation is the basic fact of all life guided her thought and research throughout her upcoming revolutionary career.

On 'Frog Lab' day, the students donned aprons and jostled for the best seats at the counters in the formaldehyde-fragrant lab. Most students looked forward to flirting and joking around in their aprons, paper hats, and plastic gloves. To a few, Frog Lab felt like an initiation into the cruelest world in school.

Still, even the most revolted of the kids looked forward to the "Day of Dissection."

Students plucked a fresh dead bullfrog from a bin and laid it on the counter top where they would work.

Some in the class cherished hands-on science. Some wanted only a good grade. Others, sincerely nauseated or simply mouthy, couldn't help declaring their disgust.

"Yuk. Do we have to?"

"This is the worst day of school."

"I'll take an F if I can go home right now!"

Mr. Clemens called, "Quiet. If you keep this up, you can go out to the Farm where you can help my friend James clean the bogs.

"Labs are cool places. Ancient. They're sacred. You could say all life is a biology lab because all life is an experiment. Remember that when you're in the school lab . It's a place to play and work and try and fail and sometimes make discoveries that can help everyone."

The entire class stared, quiet, thinking over Mr. Clemens' reframing of what the kids thought was a sort of their high school sandbox.

One of the kids raised her hand, saying, "You mean it's sacred like a church?"

"Yes. Like that. Now, who knows the most ordinary, commonest lab in the world?"

"I know!" Jade said. Other hands popped up.

"One at a time." Mr. Clemens said.

"A car repair garage!" one of the boys shouted.

"A hair salon!" a girl called out.

"A library!" the class poet said.

Mr. Clemens raised his hand for quiet. He said, "Jade."

She glanced up at him, then dropped her eyes to her desk.

"Please tell us your thought."

Jade was not a biology scholar like many others and rarely spoke in class.

"It's probably wrong but ...."

Mr. Clemens raised his eyebrows and smiled, nodding for her to continue.

“The kitchen. My mom and dad and me are always experimenting with new recipes and

changing regular ones. We mess up a lot, but,” she said with a note of triumph in her soft voice, “sometimes we cook a dish nobody can resist!”

“Right!” Mr. Clemens tossed her a double thumbs up. “The kitchen is the commonest most productive lab in every culture. It’s the first human invention and the source of all progress and joy and health in society.”

The class mumbled and shuffled around, crinkling their paper aprons.

“What do we say when we’re making progress or doing a fun thing, like making music or winning a game.”

“We’re good.”

“We got it.”

“We’re hot.”

Jade raised her hand.

“Speak up, Jade,” Mr. Clemens encouraged.

“How about, ‘we’re cookin’?”

“That’s it,” Mr. Clemens said. “We’re cookin!”

“We’re cookin’, we’re cookin’, we’re cooking,” the class chanted.

“Okay,” the master biologist said. “One cautionary story before we get started.”

The class was impatient to start dissecting. Lots of Mr. Clemens’ stories were dumb, but sometimes they were fun so they agreed.

Mr. Clemens grinned. “You’ll like this one. This happened a while back. A boy decided he was a chef. He caught one of the big Frog Frolic bullfrogs and brought it into the lab one day after school. He was alone and he locked the lab door. He filled a beaker with water, fired up a Bunsen burner on high, put the water on the burner. When it boiled, he plopped in the living frog.

"As the water warmed, he watched the frog paddle faster and faster, trying to escape. He was curious about how long it would take to 'cook': Just then, the boy heard noises in the hall. A teacher or the janitor, or who knows.

"He freaked out. Turned out the lab lights and waited. The person outside stopped, tried the door. When they found it locked, they rattled it, then walked away.

"The boy quickly unlocked the door, went into the hall, locked the door behind him. Just as he was sneaking off, the principal came around the corner.

"Sam," she said. "What are you doing in the lab."

Sam stopped in his tracks. "Nothing. Nothing," he said.

The principal glared at him.

"A little experiment," he muttered.

"Let's take a look," she said, unlocking the door. "Come on."

Sam followed her in.

"O my god," she said.

The beaker had cracked and broken, the shards laying in a puddle of water, a dead frog splayed on the tabletop. The Bunsen burner was flaming away.

Sam rushed to shut off the gas to the burner. He picked up a towel and began to mop up the water.

"Forget it, Sam," the principal said. "You could have burned down the school! I can't believe it."

"I didn't mean it. I was just doing an experiment. Teacher said that's how we learn. Try and fail and try again."

The principal shook her head, staring at him. “This was not an experiment, Sam. It was pure stupidity. Go home. Bring your parents in at 8:30 in the morning. Don’t plan on doing any more of your experiments.”

Mr. Clemens paused. As he gazed out the window he asked the class. “What do you think happened next?”

Nobody volunteered.

“He got suspended from his classes for two weeks. His coach had to kick him off the track team. He could come back to school on the condition he would leave school every day two minutes after his last class. If he did anything stupid like that again, he could be expelled.”

After a moment of shifting around, aprons rustling in the class’s discomfort, a kid said, “Did he get to take the frog home for supper?”

Weak laughter arose. Mr. Clemens ignored it.

“Who knows my first name?”

Everybody raised their hands.

“Samuel,” the new girl, Priti, said.

“Yup. That was me. I almost burned down the school when I was 16. If my parents hadn’t grounded me for a month, I probably wouldn’t have graduated.”

The class had never heard that story. They gawked at Mr. Clemens.

“I don’t have to tell you the lesson of that story.”

Kids shook their heads, agreeing.

Then Kai, an up-and-coming class comic, raised his hand and said, “If you’re here by yourself, don’t unlock the door when you hear the principal coming.”

“No, no,” a serious student said. “Don’t be stupid.”

Will, in his boundless self-importance, said, "Did you get to eat the frog?"

The class hissed and booed.

"Don't be an idiot like Will."

"You're a loser, Will."

"We should boil you!"

"Grow up."

A few of Will's friends made eating and gagging motions. He shrugged.

Mr. Clemens stared at Will, frowning, exhaling hard, said, "You all. Don't screw around in the lab! Lesson learned?"

"Yeah."

"We got it."

"Can we dissect the frogs now?"

The class moved around, chatting, somed of boys juking, conversations fluttering around the lab as Mr. Clemens' self-revelation settled in.

"Okay, class. It's lab time. Let's get cookin'!"

The class groaned and raised their blades, ready to slice. Mr. Clemens watched three kids handle their scalpels with more than normal confidence. He'd seen scars on their arms now hidden under long sleeves.

After the squawking stopped, ignoring the students who pinched their noses, he waved a scalpel back and forth and up and down like a symphony director.

"Just so you know, it's true, some frogs can regrow their legs. But don't expect that from your amputations of cadavers today.

"Pick up your scalpels. Follow me. A big part of your

grade will depend on orderliness. If you make a mess the first time you slice and dice, we have plenty of deceased *Rainidaes* you can practice on."

"It's cruel, man. Killing all those frogs just so we can cut 'em up," someone would say. "How do you off 'em anyway?"

When the kids poked into the clump of limp frogs, some legs would twitch. "Eeee. They're still alive!"

A kid would pick one up, wave it around, prop its mouth open in front of his face, croak. The class would dissolve in laughing.

Mumbles and exclamations and cheers sounded in the room as the class members tried to follow Mr. Clemens incisions. He waited for the inevitable contest to arise among the party prone.

It usually started with a boy holding up and stretching a frog tongue, shouting, "Mine is bigger than yours."

Half the class would cut the tongues out of their specimens, raising them, waving them around.

"Bacon. Look at my bacon," one the most immature boys would holler, feeling license to act out to get attention.

"Dim. Stupid. Idiot," sneered some girls.

"It's long and pink and fatty," the boy would say.

"Yours looks like a tiny piece of chewed up bubble gum," a girl would declare.

Her friends howled. Students doubled over laughing and hooting. The humiliated boy would be saddled with the nickname "Bacon" for the rest of the week.

At the end of the term and Mr. Clemens' demanding papers and exams, if no student earned less than a B-, and none did, Biology concluded with the most memorable class of the high school years.

With a straight face and a serious tone, Mr. Clemens introduced the topic of frog reproduction by saying, "Class, now we're going to talk about the purpose of every life – procreation."

Giggles and snorts from the kids.

"Or, as they say at Frog Frolic, *The Spawning*. That means laying eggs. Don't snigger. Amphibian love is what supports our town. For you wordsmiths, here's the word of the day: *amplexus*."

Mumbling spread from desk to desk as mock bullfrog barks and tree frog trills rose and fell and rose in rhythm.

Mr. Clemens ignored these outbursts and used them to build dramatic tension in the room. At a well-rehearsed point in his ten-minute lecture on the conditions in ponds and swamps and woodlands necessary for frog spawning, he would notice students' anticipation peaking.

Mr. Clemens projected a slide on the wall, and said, "You all know what's next," he said, looking over his glasses at the class.

"Amplexus," hollered a boy. Echoes of "Amplexus. Amplexus," rang through the room.

"You have a wonderful vocabulary," Mr. Clemens scowled in jest, he said turning to the projector.

"*The male frog clasps the female.*"

The boys hooted and hollered and stomped the floor. Some of the girls turned their eyes down, while others rolled their eyes at the boys.

"Clasp. I can remember that!" said a boy in the back row. "*Clasp you*, dude!"

Mr. Clemens continued. "The lady frog releases her eggs, the guy frog fertilizes them, and pretty soon, tadpoles!"

Since the time Mr. Clemens showed the slide in his first year of teaching, whenever a graduate of his class wanted to get another's attention, the "c-word" replaced the "f-word".

"Okay," Mr. Clemens said. "That's it. No more rowdiness. Show some respect – to the frogs. Class dismissed."

New Hopes

Kermit, leapers, phantasmals, splashbacks

During the school's 'Frog Day' every spring, each class participated in a "Name That Frog" contest. The winner was a student who could both identify the most frogs by their particular calls and draw an accurate depiction of them. Tree frogs didn't count because their liquid notes could be recognized and often mimicked by most children before they could talk.

Students teamed up with their best friends to compete in the raucous Leap Frog tournament. The farthest leapers and the funniest frog costumes won certificates.

The entire school population and parents turned out to cheer on the contestants and laugh till their stomachs hurt at the kids' costumes and antics.

Over the years, students' drawings and sculptures of myriad frogs filled a lit wall display in the main foyer. The art carried titles like "Miniature Iridescent Teardrops," "Finned Frog Racers," "Backward-leaping Frogs," "Bucking Bronco Frogs," "Elkhorn Frogs."

Every year activist students lobbied the school to fund a frog film with audio accessible at the press of a button.

And every year, the penny-pinching school board denied the request, saying "Just go outside!"

The kids had studied the Mark Twain story "The Celebrated Jumping Frog of Calaveras County." Teachers didn't deny the Frog Frolic Farm claim that Twain visited the original Frog Frolic ponds where he was struck with the idea for the story. By the time the kids had graduated, their general knowledge of frogs exceeded their knowledge of almost any other subject except their native language.

The high school social studies curriculum included a college credit course in *Kermit: His Deception of Children and Adults*. An elective course in English, *The Meaning of the Golden Ball in the Princess and Frog Prince Tale*, attracted the SpecFic and FanFic writers.

Any kid could enroll in either or both classes, but only those with high grades and excellent recommendations from the teacher could qualify for the annual senior class trip to the wild swamps of Louisiana to research Kermit's birthplace. Unfounded but widely believed rumors about the uninhibited behaviors allowed to those selected seniors gave rise to stiff competition for the twenty-three slots available.

Fortunately for the students, the high school was so small the senior class rarely had twenty-three students. The years when class numbers exceeded twenty-three, the administration usually changed the number of openings so all seniors could earn good grades and qualify for the trip of their lifetimes.

Virtual visits to the American Museum of Natural History in New York and other museums around the world were popular pastimes for grandparents and their grandkids.

As a primary schooler, Rosa had logged into the Museum's site to take tours and courses and play games. She begged her parents to become members and take her to New York so she could see everything without a screen in between her and the displays.

One Saturday afternoon, after she'd studied the amphibian pages for the third time, she said to her dad, Carlos, "Do you know why there are so many frog species in the world?"

"Because they're slimy and ugly and nobody wants to touch them."

"No way."

"Because humans like to gig 'em for bait or eat frog legs?"

"Be serious, papa. They evolved because they are so beautiful. That's what the Museum says."

"Okay. Well, *mija* knows what the museum knows," her dad said.

Rosa laughed. "Look at this." She typed a long URL into her tablet.

"What are doing?" Carlos asked.

"Just wait. It's a website. *www.amnh.org/exhibitions/frogs-a-chorus-of-colors/the amazing adaptable frog.*" She set the tablet on the arm of his chair.

Carlos gazed at the images. "Amazing. They are gorgeous. Nothing like those bullfrogs the Farm raises."

"Papa, they're all cousins!" she scolded. "Every single one is beautiful."

"Yes, *mija,*" Carlos said, scrolling through the site. "They're wonderful. I see why you care so much about them.

"Did you know the coqui frog is the national animal of Puerto Rico?"

"Of course, papa. Mi Abuela played a record of their songs to me when I was a little kid and couldn't sleep. She said they were her lullaby when she was a little girl, too."

"I'll always love their songs," Carlos said. "B'beep! B'beep! B'beep!"

Rosa laughed and joined her dad in a coqui duet.

As part of the Frog Day festival, the Farm sponsored a frog jumping contest. Unlike in Twain's Calaveras County, cheating wasn't allowed, so it was pure luck that determined the winning frog.

Frog farmers attached numbers to the backs of random frogs plucked from the ponds and the kids picked a frog's number from a hat. They set their frogs down behind a line and waited. The winner was the frog that jumped the furthest in the first five minutes of the contest.

One of the most popular activities was the town's form of racetrack betting, only the animals were frogs. The winning gambler came closest to guessing the actual distance the longest leaper leapt.

The total betting pool could reach thousands of dollars because, win or lose, the funds went to support the Leap Frog Tournament and the festivities.

The Tournament was always the most boisterous event of the day. Bettors screamed and yelled for their frogs and stamped on the ground behind them.

"Go, seventeen!"

"Come on, twenty-six!"

"Harry, pick it up!"

"Westy, move it. Don't be a sluggard!"

"Fifty-five! You can do it!"

The elders who had won as children passed down their wisdom, but no trick or name or wish made a difference in the frog-jumping champion. Every frog was a long shot.

Everyone agreed on the fact that the largest frogs or the loudest croakers were not the farthest leapers. The Farm had tried to breed champion leapers for the contest, but the furthest leapers always came from the haphazard choices the farmers made the day of the contest.

The centerpiece of Frog Day was a raucous parade with floats vying for awards. The funniest, the most imaginative, the prettiest. Kids and adults dressed in colorful frog costumes hopped and danced around.

Accompanied by chiming triangles, bleating harmonicas, and a loud chorus of barkers and croakers, the kids sang frog songs they'd composed.

Every year pairs of best friends in drama class dressed as Frog and Toad and acted out their favorite episodes from the famous books.

When an adult-sized Kermit the Frog rode down Bullfrog Avenue on a lily leaf float, lucky kids rode along and tossed out frog-shaped hard candies and little metal frog clickers to the audience cheering from the curbs.

Some kids collected dozens of clickers, scavenging them from under cars and abandoned in gutters. They formed groups to click beats and chant "Ribbit! Ribbit! Ribbit!" to their parents' annoyance.

The police, decked out in a variety of Frogwoman and Frogman outfits, patrolled the fringes of the parade.

They didn't have much to do except peer through their swimming goggles and croak or ribbit and leap in clumsy hops across the street. When the police flopped and flapped and splatted the street with their so-called frog feet encased in swim fins, young children scattered and hid behind their laughing parents' legs. Older kids and some adults squatted and croaked and hopped around the police.

The Frog Marching Band, composed of adults eighteen to eighty-seven, highlighted the parade. Drummers beat on different sizes of plastic buckets – the largest buckets resonated like bullfrogs, the middle-sized buckets popped with the steady popcorn beat of mink frogs, while the smallest pails pinged with the bouncing *chip chip chip* of green frogs.

The jaw harp section of the band vibrated and planged.

Ancient washboards, saved since the old days just for the parade, screeched. A hopping team of penny whistlers played the high-pitched call of tiny gray tree frogs. Bass guitars underscored the whole production with deep hums.

After the parade, some kids chosen for their tidiness in class, dusted and mopped the Frog Museum. It was about the only time of year anyone visited the museum. For one thing, the stuffed colorful and toxic frogs from around the world were old and saggy. The poison dart red *Splashbacks*' skin had faded to a dull blood clot color. The Harlequins' once elegant costumes were dingy and dull. The *Phantasmals* looked like globs of mud.

Visitors usually passed by the plump, mounted remains of the giant bullfrog, once fifteen inches from nose to tail. When they did notice the shape tucked in the shadow under a fern, they assumed it was a small clump of *papier maché* mud.

The only semi-controversial display was the room that featured a mural depicting the evolution of humanity from one-celled creatures. Where organic life progressed through selective breeding and inter-species cooperation and competition from cells to plants to fish to the reptiles and amphibians, several species of frog were painted and buffed to show patterns as unique and changeable as clouds at sunrise.

One local church forbade their children from looking at the evolution mural, but the other churches, the mosque and the synagogue encouraged field trips every year. Predictably, on the annual middle school trip, raucous boys snickered and joked about selective breeding.

The most ardent biology students loved the notion of random change and the paradoxes of evolution, learning that nature didn't reward only the so-called "fittest individuals" with survival, but the most cooperative. The beauty, diversity, and complexity of the natural world led many to major in biology, ecology, and pre-med in college.

Once the most popular display in the museum, "Fluorescent Frogs," it was now the most disappointing. In the old days, when kids and families had to line up and wait to enter the room until another group came out, twenty-four species of ghostly bioluminescent frogs and a dozen night-gleaming salamanders from around the world gleamed and shone.

"Ooos" and "ahhhs" and giggles cascaded from the room exciting the waiting group's expectations.

When they entered, the visitors picked up blue light flashlights and made their way around the dark room, aiming the light at the frogs luminescing with every mottled color in the spectrum from shimmering lavender and sparkling emerald- green to bewitching scarlet.

Over time, the frog and salamander skin cells lost their brilliance and neither blue nor infrared nor any other light could revive the magical luminous glows.

Replacing the bioluminescent frogs became too expensive for the museum so the "Fluorescent Frogs" room faded into happy childhood memories of the museum's older visitors.

Except for the special room with the mural and the "Fluorescent Frogs" room, most adults and all children found the rest of the museum's crumbling fake environments and old frog videos boring. Instead, they went outside to listen to live frog hullabaloo happening all around.

Whenever Rosa felt blue from bickering with her mom or hearing nasty words from her classmates or missing her grandfather or just about anything that made her feel bad, she thought of the mural and evolution.

Knowing she was one of an infinite number of beings on earth, all connected, comforted her, reminding her that a sad feeling would pass and be absorbed into a happy sense of the beautiful oneness of everything, no matter how blue she felt. After one of her solitary visits to the museum, she told Mr. Clemens about her peaceful feeling.

He said, “I know. I feel the same.”

“When I told Simmi,” Rosa said, “she said she feels that way when she gets up early to watch the sunrise.”

“I wish everybody felt it,” Mr. Clemens said. “It feels sacred.”

After a few seconds, Rosa placed her palms together in prayer position, feeling a little like her grandmother. She pointed her hands as Mr. Clemens and, smiling, nodded her head.

Mr. Clemens grinned and bowed his head to Rosa.

Then they laughed.

New music

After a while, with the frogs gone silent, the townspeople realized how they'd depended on the frogs in more ways than just for jobs at the Farm and cash flowing through the town businesses and services.

For some residents, frog song inspired their spiritual lives, hearing the frog chorus as angelic. A pantheistic bunch felt the earth was talking to them in Gaia's voice, assuring them the goddess was watching over the world with her eternal caring.

Frog weather forecasting was an art passed from generation to generation, usually from a grandparent to a grandchild. A universal belief among the citizens held that, on any day, the length, pace, and pitch of frog calls could predict the weather.

Amateur meteorologists had collected data comparing the changes in weather with the day-by-day measures of the beginnings and endings of peak croaks and warbles. After making daily recording of sounds at the ponds, the citizen scientists developed colorful charts to show the correlations to different kinds of weather.

Frog silence belied the traditional forecasts and the spreadsheets became irrelevant.

The modern prognosticators brainstormed ways to come up with new ways to predict weather without frogs' voice rhythms. The most dedicated weather people observed the growth of algae, the number of frogs visible above the water at certain sites, and the growth rate of cattails.

Town educators worried about the intellectual effects of The Silence since it was common knowledge that listening to frog song since they were born made the town's children smarter than the kids who didn't grow up in a sound shower of frog music. The evidence was clear. The town kids won more music contests, debates, and science shows than students in the other schools of the same size across the state.

Children learned to count by listening to frogs and calling out their numbers in the cadence of bullfrog croaks. At the library kids produced stop motion videos with hand-made frog puppets. The shows became Community TV and YouTube favorites.

Even though the town had a critical economic investment in the frogs, and despite general Chamber of Commerce enthusiasm, not everyone was happy with the frogs, let alone what some felt was dreary non-stop warbling and chirping and croaking.

Some claimed frog calls were depressing animal babel. Others hated the swampy odors drifting into town so much they sealed their houses against the reek. They wore earplugs when they were anywhere near the Farm to protect themselves from the irritating frog chatter.

"There's no damn symphony there," the neighbors said.

"It's pure chaos," maintained others who heard no music or harmonies.

The most typical frog song detesters also complained about the appearance of common frogs. They agreed that some are colored and pretty, especially the poison ones, but most are downright "muck-ugly."

Early in The Silence, despite the electronic clatter of nightly hour-long broadcast of recorded frog calls from the public address speakers on the town common, most townspeople were optimistic, always believing The Silence would pass.

A few months into The Silence, a spate of tree frog calls rang and pinged into the nights. During the next two weeks most people in town relaxed.

"See? No worries. They're coming back," was the common upbeat outlook.

As suddenly as they erupted, the tree frog trills stopped.

Kids learned that tree frogs hide in tiny alcoves using the surrounding bark to amplify their songs. They searched the edges of the ponds and into the wetlands where some found the wee beings.

Lucky kids found an abundance of the frogs hiding under leaves and in the bark. They picked them up, stroked or shook them hoping to elicit a trill or chirp. The frogs ignored their handlers.

Soon, all chirping faded away except for an occasional blurt or two just after dusk.

Loss of incessant frog chittering and chiming and squawking brought the townsfolk an unexpected gift. With their frog-call sensitized ears, they picked up sounds they hadn't heard since they were infants.

The tender brushing of leaves in light breeze, subtle overtones in conversational voices, the distant pop of screen doors slamming several blocks away.

On drizzly days, the sounds of the droplets bouncing off the leaves or pinging on the water relaxed anyone nearby. When it rained, the citizens loved the feeling of being swathed in soothing sound – buckets, torrents, pours, deluges, thunderstorms.

On clear days, without interference from frog calls, people noticed the gentle buzzing of bees in the gardens and distant calls of owls and songs of birds they'd never heard before.

Some children said they could hear the pecking of robins and juncos in the grass. Other kids reported being able to hear blossoms unfolding.

Rosa and her friends began to whisper, challenging each other to repeat aloud exactly what others had voiced. Mumbled singing became popular, if dubious, in rousing otherwise silent church worship.

Elders waxed wistful. Many missed naming the calls of a dozen different species, singling them out from the usual boring cluster of barking and chirping.

Early risers agreed they wished they could hear the ticking of the tiniest frogs every day just before dawn.

The LFA offered to design an app, "Frog Songs." Much like a bird or plant ID app, Frog Songs invited researchers from around the world to record, identify, and submit the sounds of the frogs.

Students in US university herpetology programs networked around the country to compare and contrast chirps, barks, whistles, and every note of frog sounds they could fine. Soon, submissions from Nigeria, South Africa and many others began to expand the app.

To relieve their refreshed aural appetites, more than a few townspeople perfected their guitar chords and ukulele strums. Mouth harpists accompanied by flutists mimicked bullfrog calls and tree frogs' warbles. Pianists played Bach concertos for neighborhood gatherings. Gray-haired five-gallon bucket thumpers recorded themselves pounding and calling and posted their performances on YouTube.

Some non-musical jokesters claimed they'd found a natural and common solution to the loss of frog refrains with no talent needed – listening to the chirping of crickets in their yards and basements.

The trains passing along the edge of town four times every day became a popular listening and social event. Starting at five fifty-five a.m. and repeating every six hours, residents set up their camp chairs near the tracks to listen to the trains for the ten minutes it took to roll by. Each scheduled time had its own coterie of listeners who became experts at train sounds.

The "Breakfast Club," early risers who daily showed up at the coffee shop, now made their first stop of the morning at the tracks. One of the men, a retired railroad switchman, knew several of the locomotive engineers. When he waved, his engineer friends gave the horn a long whistle and a double toot.

The sharpest ears could identify the faint hum of the tracks when the incoming trains were still miles outside of town and again as it clanged away out of sight.

Even citizens with average hearing learned to differentiate among the rattles and bangs of oil trains, coal trains, container trains. Easiest of all to discern were the squeals and clunks of noontime Amtrak cars.

Eventually, interest in socializing 'down at the tracks' waned for all but the most insomniac of the Breakfast Club. A few early rising widows and widowers sometimes showed up to see who of their age group was still energetic and curious, and who might become a new bridge partner or fellow walker.

As time passed, a profound and obvious question circulated among the shops and the grocery stores: "If they don't croak, how can the frog boys and girls find each other to mate?"

New theories and jokes arose. "Telepathy" was popular. "Body language" was a common scientific opinion. The refrain of a popular high school rap song went "They squat and they hop and they hop till they stop and they bop, bop, bop."

The most empathetic types in town wondered if frogs love to sing and talk to each other just like people.

"It's fundamental," they said. "It's their poetry, their romance. They love the sounds of their own voices, like us."

"Like all animals," they added.

Rosa listened to the theories. She knew in her heart some could be right, though most were too strange to be believed.

The telepathy idea made sense to Rosa. She'd observed that sometimes people didn't have to talk to know what the other person wanted. When she asked her mother about it, she said, "Rosa, sometimes it's just something in the air."

Right then, Rosa decided to learn just what that something was.

Since nobody could answer how the frogs could find mates during The Silence, a slight existential doubt about the future of the Farm and of the town enveloped the citizens.

New conspiracy theories arose – a coterie of witches had cast a spell, foreign agents had secretly infected the bogs with gene-distorting viruses, the government was testing biological warfare weapons, crossbreeding of frogs had created silent monsters who could contaminate humans and make them mute.

Such fears moved some residents to the edge of nature mysticism.

They adopted as their spiritual leader Si'ahl, known as Chief Seattle, quoting his poignant words, "What is life if a person can't hear the voices of the frogs around the pond at night."

Citizens who had moved to the town from the northern states showed equanimity in The Silence. Natives attributed the northern immigrants' peace of mind to their being raised in snow country where the quiet solaced and romanced their winter minds.

On a lighter note, Olivia, the mayor's eleven year old granddaughter, sighed, "I love the frogs. They're cute. I don't care if they don't peep or croak. They're so sweet."

"Yeah," her brother Jayden said. "Silent frogs are still magic. They have superpowers. They're shape changers. First, they're fish with fins, then they're four-leggers with webby fingers."

Feral media and the GMOMs

Eventually, word of the mute frogs flew across the internet sparking a media conflagration of stories about what they considered a hilarious situation.

Headlines blared and flew.

"Croak and Dagger in Frog Town."

"Frogs Frolic and Feed on Frosted Flies."

"Scientists investigate possible immortality gene in frog throats – they never croak!"

"Chaos in Kermitville!"

Stupid frog jokes became de rigueur on late night shows and popular with young kids.

"What do you get when you cross a frog and a dog? A Croaker Spaniel."

"What sort of shoes do frogs wear? Open-toad sandals."

"Why didn't the frog sit on the toadstool? Because there wasn't mushroom."

Advertising capitalized on frog humor. "What's a frog's favorite place to eat? IHOP."

"What's a frog's favorite drink? Croak-a-Cola."

Dozens of videos with people dressed as frogs hopping

around and splashing in shallow ponds swam across the vast swamps of social media.

Instagram and YouTube frog people pretended party favor blowouts were their frog tongues, stretching, withdrawing, stretching, withdrawing. Varieties of green blowouts that croaked or chirped when people blew into them to unfurl the paper tubes became a popular toy.

Facebook Frogs groups sprouted, spreading news of The Silence. The mayor's website crashed due to thousands of tweeted remedies proposed by both serious scientists and sarcastic jokesters.

The treatments from the mockers and cruel crowd ranged from "Pinch 'em" to "scare 'em with a flock of ducks" to "quick freeze 'em and thaw 'em in microwaves. That'll jolt 'em into croaking one way or the other – hahaha."

Most townsfolk shrugged off the comments. The Chamber of Commerce president said, "Hey, any publicity is good publicity."

Still, humiliation at the hands of the media weighed heavy on the psyches of many.

Those with social media savvy took to the internet to hush the sarcasm and invigorate digital affection for frogs.

A teacher tweeted several times a day for a month some snippets of the *Frog and Toad* series of new reader books. Demand for the printed books, especially among home schoolers, shot up. As the word spread, Amazon was forced to provide three new printings before the demand returned to normal.

The town writers' group wrote an encomium to frogs and published it everywhere. The town poet posted a sign in his front yard with his translation of the famous haiku by Basho.

LFAers swarmed the internet with videos of frogs leaping and diving, croaking, calling, and clasping. Thousands of still photos of the most colorful and endangered species were downloaded by teachers and kids of all ages around the world.

Someone resuscitated the ancient arcade video game, Frogger. Modernizing it with 3-D software and life-like characters, they made a free app named "Frogger Redux" that became one of the month's top downloads.

Mr. Clemens posted an outline of his high school frog biology curriculum and offered to consult with anyone who wanted to teach about the frog world.

The upbeat news lasted a few days on the peak of the remorseless unbreaking media surf. The poetry became rewritten and mocked but made into several songs, all of which had ringtoneable frog croak beats. The town writers didn't know whether to raise their voices in hallelujah or to smile at their prescience.

The popular jokes resumed circulation. The most common joke among many was "What did the frog dress up as on Halloween? A prince."

The second most popular was "What happened when the frog's car broke down?"

"He got toad."

Within a few months, the media hoopla settled back into the same weary quiet as the frog bogs.

About that time Dr. Yvette, now living in Thailand, found celebrity as a frog defender. She published a blog piece describing the frogs' unique power among animals, echoing the pleasure and insights frogs brought to children. She noted how frogs had inspired her to a deeper understanding of the miracles life holds. She also published a few of her favorite frog recipes.

After she read her posts, Rosa reached out to Dr. Yvette. "Doc, I have a weird idea," she texted. "Just between us. If it gets out, I'm afraid people will go nuts."

Doc texted back. "The weirder the better."

"What if our frogs have been eating those genetically modified mosquitos they released? They could have blown up here from Florida and affected the frogs' genes."

"I doubt it. Only a few bug genes were modified. Still, it's a good idea. I'll set up a study.

Doc's agreement thrilled Rosa. The famous frog scientist thought she'd had a good idea!

She emailed Rosa two months later. "No indications of GMOM (mosquitos) outside the original range. 2. I've fed GMOMs to hundreds of frogs. They all croak and trill."

"Whew," Rosa emailed back. "What about the tads? Maybe the damage is done years before the frogs mature?"

"Yes. It would be a long-term research project. I'll let you know."

"Thank you."

"Keep thinking, Rosa."

"Can't stop that. Except about the mean things people say on media."

"There are some people who think being stupid is funny," Dr. Yvette wrote. "The joke will be on them!"

Rosa wrote back, "I guess. Here's my latest idea. The silent frogs are a brand new species!!!"

Dr. Yvette replied immediately. "Good idea. Somebody should do that research. Unfortunately, research costs money. The GMOMs are using most of my money."

"Can't you get some more?" Rosa asked.

A few days later, Rosa received an answer from Doc.

"The funders don't care about frogs unless you could change them into some kind of AI pollution watchers."

"They already are that, except organic." Rosa insisted.

"Keep thinking, Rosa. You'll find something positive about your silent frogs."

That was the last time Rosa heard from her for years.

The frog princess

In spired by The Silence, the high school drama club and a collaboration of musicians and rappers rewrote Arnold Lobel's Broadway musical "A Year with Frog and Toad." They performed it to rowdy, overflow crowds in the school auditorium.

Middle schoolers now, Rosa and her friends Shondie and Xandra played sneaky foxes. They stumbled and flopped around, mimicking frogs hopping. Their comedy routine was the hit of Act Two.

After the show, the mayor, Mrs. Gould, announced the contest to name the town's Frog Princess and host the annual town party. The program would add levity and boost the spirits of the townspeople, the mayor hoped.

The town council spread a rumor alleging the University Science department hypothesized that the upcoming Frog Princess jamboree might, just might, spark the magical return of the frog song.

Most considered that silly but decided to go along. The mayor followed up the rumor with the caveat that no matter what happens, everyone would have a good time.

Primary school teachers used the festival as an opportunity to have the students practice their cursive. The children wrote letters to everyone they knew in town and all their far-flung relatives inviting them to a fairy tale festival. The post office sold out the entire U.S. Postal Service district supply of Forever frog stamps.

Middle School students drew and painted princesses with golden balls and plump frogs posed on the lips of wells. They printed posters with their art and displayed them in friendly merchants' windows.

The winner of the princess role was chosen. Esme, a pretty but often hapless girl who, surprised at her luck, accepted the title, anticipating popularity and a change for the better in her life.

Jorge, the high school track team's long-jumper, was named the Frog Prince. He scrounged in the drama department's costume closet until he found a foil crown. He propped it on his head, wearing it like a prince, swaggering and grinning when classmates teased him.

"Yo, Prince of the Swamps."

"Show us your hops, bro!"

Jorge obliged. He backed off, ran hard, and leapt and hopped.

Officially, Esme was named the "Princess of Music," but everyone called her "The Frog Princess." Unlike Jorge, she took her role seriously, believing the rumor that the play could magically bring back the frogs' songs.

As time passed between her award and the event, she had to ignore endless jokes from kids in her class. She heard about any number of frog princes who couldn't change out of their froggy skin.

As the day approached, Esme just wanted to get it over with. Since her dad was a second-generation frog farmer and it meant a lot to him, she gritted her teeth and donned the costume.

Townspeople gathered on a brilliant sunny day in Newt Park, the town's public gathering place near Frog Frolic Farm ponds. Esme perched on a high-backed chair painted gold to look like a throne.

Wearing a purple velvet robe and jeweled rhinestone crown her mom had ordered online, she waved her wand in one hand and tossed a tennis ball spray-painted gold up and down in her other hand, reigning over a crowd of youth and their parents. Jorge waited behind the boulders the Department of Public Works had arranged to stand in for the frog's well.

Enthralled by the day's rituals, families and curious visitors to town stood on the edge of Amber Pond, their eyes wide, their ears peeled, holding their breath, hoping to hear at least a tree frog trill or a bullfrog bark.

A young and handsome farmhand, dressed in tux and tie, picked up a 'magical' blue, red, and yellow striped frog and toted it on a silver platter to the girl.

When the duded-up frog farmer presented the plate of the hidden Prince, Esme grimaced and pinched her nose.

She considered the damp frog, recalling how the meanest girls had laughed and said over and over, "At least you'll get to kiss somebody, even if it is a frog."

With the crowd staring at her and kids chanting "Kiss it. Kiss it. Kiss it," her stomach ached and a sour taste formed in her mouth. Esme couldn't take it.

She wretched and choked out "I hate you. This is so fu ... fu ... clasped ... fucked up!"

Tears sliding down her cheeks, she leapt down from her throne, ripped off her crown, and sailed it into the crowd. She threw down the gold tennis ball and her wand and lurched away, shouting "You're so mean! Fuck you!"

Jorge popped out from behind the rocks calling "Esme. Wait. You can kiss me instead!"

She stopped, turned to look at him. A long moment passed as she stopped and stared.

Esme tossed her head, shouting, "No way. I'd rather kiss a frog!"

Jorge's friends laughed and jeered him, until the mayor called, "Be quiet. You're acting like children!"

Esme's mother ran after her as Esme disappeared behind the equipment garage. Her mother found her sobbing and tearing off her princess garb. They hugged, sitting down until Esme stopped crying.

"You should never have let them make me kiss a frog!" Esme accused her mother. "Nobody loves me."

Back at the pond, some of the crowd, taken aback by Esme's reaction, closed around her father who stood dumbfounded, asking him how they could help.

He told them that Esme was never sure she wanted to be Frog Princess. Esme had endured the cruel jokes of her classmates and how sensitive she was.

When Esme's dad's friends heard that, they recalled their own wisecracks and callous jokes they'd made about their own high school frog princesses.

Several people glanced around, caught another's eye, and looked down at their feet. After a moment of quiet, a woman's voice rose.

"That's awful," she called out. "She's a sweet kid." When she had the attention of the crowd, she went on. "We don't need to make jokes about our children, what with the whole claspin' internet doing it to all of us!"

Mayor Gould raised her bullhorn.

"Okay, folks. Listen up," she said. "Esme, can you hear

me? We're sorry. The whole town apologizes to you and your whole family."

"Yeah!"

"Right."

"We're sorry, Esme."

"Come back. We'll be nice!"

"We need you."

Esme stayed hidden behind the building.

Chagrined, her dad shrugged and hurried away to join his wife and daughter.

Mayor Gould had weathered countless municipal crises and political storms over the years. She knew she had to distract and humor the people. She had to eliminate the shame and anger her constituents felt.

Sighing, frowning, her lips turned down in sadness, Mayor Gould picked up the princess crown and placed it on her head. Facing the crowd, she said, "I nominate myself to be Frog Princess this year. I didn't get to when I was young."

Grinning, she scooped up the frog and displayed it to the crowd. She exhaled and kissed the frog.

A child spoke into the quiet. "Mama, is she eating that frog?"

Wiping off her lips with her handkerchief, the mayor said to Jorge. "Come back, Prince. Bring that golden ball. Let's go to the castle."

Jorge picked up the ball where Esme had thrown it and trudged toward the mayor, his face red and pinched with embarrassment. The audience let a few chuckles slip, but no one heard a peep from the frogs.

The mayor said, “Thank you, Jorge. You can go.” To the crowd she said, “Fellow citizens. Thank you for your attendance. Let’s be patient. There’s thousands of species of frogs in the world. We’ll import some noisy ones. They’ll mate with the silent ones and produce loud noisy croakers,” she promised.

She hoisted the frog platter and tipped the frog into the water. It hopped onto the reeds and swam.

Now the center of the spectators’ attention, it climbed onto a half-submerged tree trunk and sat in silence, a tiny gargoyle with bulging black eyes.

“It looks fine. Maybe even happy,” the mayor commented, repeating the common wisdom.

The crowd murmured. “Yeah. Mmm-hmm. They’re healthy.”

“You’re right,” said James. “I still believe it’s frog laryngitis. Give ‘em time. They’ll get better.”

Mayor Gould raised her bullhorn again. “Okay, folks. Let’s go have some lemonade and a picnic. Frog Frolic has provided a barbecue of its tastiest frog legs. Nobody should miss out on that.”

Nodding to the high school band, she said, “Let’s play, kids.”

They played and the crowd feasted, except Rosa and a few others. They’d given up eating frog meat when they were eleven.

Rosa told her family and friends, “If you want to eat something that tastes like stringy chicken, eat chicken.”

She didn't eat chicken, either.

When the videos of the mayor kissing the frog erupted into millions of views on YouTube and TikTok, countless frogs-turning-into-princes acts and songs went viral for a few days. Frog videos and jokes soon disappeared. It seemed The Silence had infected the entire frog realm on the internet.

Despite the publicity, the mayor received recognition and praise from her governmental colleagues across the state.

"You're quick. It took more than a little courage," said the mayor of the next town over.

"Beautiful act. I hope I never have to kiss a frog," said another.

The state representative texted her five grinning emojis. "You'll go down in history as the Frog Queen!"

"You showed your town how far you'd go for your people," the head of the University's political science department wrote. "I wish all politicians were as gutsy as you. Bravo!"

"Where did you send the prince?" her friend the governor ribbed. "Are you hiding him down a well somewhere?"

"He and the Princess have already made up," she said. "I saw them walking hand in hand around the ponds today."

Horace and Harry and the crows

Fifty new species of frogs arrived from around the world. The plan was to mate them with the 137 species already cultivated by the Farm. Some of the new frogs were farmed and imported from Vietnam and some were wild from the Amazon jungle. All were guaranteed to have barked, chirped, or croaked before they were shipped. All were beautiful in their own ways.

The people who raised or plucked or stole their amphibian prizes from jungle swamps and wetlands and from under the knees of faraway cypress trees promised that none of the imported frogs were poisonous or endangered.

Due to their encounters with the frog rustlers who were known liars, the farmers were dubious. They feared contaminations from the wilds, such as a gene for short, thin legs or a fungus that would foul the frogs they'd watched over for generations.

Assuming some of the wild frogs were deadly, they tested each batch for venom and infections. Fifteen groups were euthanized for possible toxicity. The farmers discovered three known endangered species.

"Maybe there's more," the inspectors reported to James. "We just don't know."

Assuming the best, and feeling pressure from the townspeople, James said, "Let 'em go. We'll take the risk." The farmers crossed their fingers and released the new frogs into the ponds.

After a few days of making frog music in their Frog Frolic ponds, sometimes even raising a hubbub for a few hours, maybe even mating, the new frogs fell silent, rousing then disappointing all the people in town.

Still, the people did not relent in their active hopefulness. "We can figure it out. Patience is what we have, so let's use it," was the common plan.

Throughout the summer and fall the citizens took turns womanning and manning pondside listening posts, 24/7.

One evening, a teenager recorded on his phone what he thought was a ribbit. Then another. Then some rattles and clicks. He took it to his friends who copied it and spread the news around town.

When the elders listened using expensive earphones, they said they could hear what sounded like tinny cricket song, but nothing froggy. After a few more weeks of bored listening, the teen listeners departed. Still, the recording boded well for what could come.

In the heavy humid days of summer, hordes of cicadas scritching and nighttime crickets shrieking formed a welcome wall of sound. The ears and minds of the suffering townspeople felt relief, even tinges of pleasure.

Citizens who were depressed by the loss of frog calls

felt reinvigorated, like themselves again. Some people sat up all night to listen. The vociferous bugs then helped the older folks drop into calm trances like the late-night frog calls that once sent them off to slumberland.

Unfortunately, the cricket stridulations irritated more citizens than they pleased.

"Those crickets are a one-horse pony. At least frogs sing with personalities."

The pharmacy and grocery store sold out of earplugs.

Fortunately for the annoyed, the incessant sawing of the crickets and cicadas lasted only a few weeks. When the insects quieted down, the shroud of silence returned.

The elders of the town were surprised by the delight many felt upon the return to The Silence. At an ecumenical meeting of the towns' spiritual leaders, they spoke for their flocks.

"Thank the stars," the pagan elder whispered.

"Thank God," the Christians of all denominations declared in unison.

"Shalom alaykam," the Mullah announced.

"Gracias a Dios, ahora y siempre," the Spanish-speaking Evangelical congregation prayed.

"Slava bogu," the Russian Orthodox priest stated.

The Buddhist monk bowed, mumbling "Om mane padme hum" three times.

The Zen monk blinked.

The town's novice shaman pounded on her drum.

"Shalom," the rabbi pronounced, smiling.

A Quaker woman stepped forward. "Beauty and peace always emerge from silence."

Satisfied they'd expressed their gratitude and shared their folds' hopes and prayers, the spiritual leaders went home.

During the dryer autumn days, some residents meeting at the Senior Center took up the cause of replacing the frog songs. With vigor and optimism, Horace and his twin brother Harry volunteered to catch and kill frogs and spread them on the streets of town to attract crows.

"Crow caws remind us of frog croaks," they said.

"Are you guys crazy or just demented," their friends joked.

"Crows are bad omens."

"Crows cackling everywhere?"

"We have enough troubles, no sweet frog tunes to help us sleep."

James, always a good citizen and smart businessman, appreciated Horace and Harry's idea. He said Frog Frolic would help. They slaughtered two hundred frogs and laid them on the side street near the Senior Center.

For a few days, watching frog carcasses became a

compulsive activity for the seniors. The twins cheered whenever crows landed and fed.

Soon, a few large crows shrieking and swooping and barking drove off the smaller ones. In corvid rage, they flew at the faces of hopeful cats. Without distraction, the biggest birds fed on the day's pickings. The few shredded frogs left over on the street at dusk disappeared by morning.

Horace and Harry shrugged. "We tried," they said.

"It was a decent idea," Ida, Harry's girlfriend, said.

"You guys kept us entertained," Dolores, Ida's twin and Harry's paramour, said, winking at Horace.

At first frost, the winter season's portion of the frog population disappeared into the mud, or, that's what the citizens hoped.

The frog farmers scooped up random samples of silt and soil and nodded to the boss and the anxious mayor, "Yup. They'll be fine. They're taking their winter snoozes. "

Visitors

The local faiths decided to hold candlelight vigils and prayer circles at the ponds. When the lights and prayers failed to summon the usual sunset choir of frogs, the ministers and rabbi and priest and mullah joined together in a radical move.

Setting aside certain lifelong beliefs, the mayor and the town council reached out to spiritual leaders from anywhere. In their desperation, they agreed to accept pagan practitioners if they passed the leaders' vetting.

In an ecumenical spirit, the congregations and parishes and mosques and synagogues and pantheists and atheists offered to host holy people of any persuasion.

Revered practitioners from all over the world arrived and offered prayers and rituals and jama'ahs and chants. The human praise songs were to give nature the spiritual charge needed to evoke frog mating calls.

A preacher from the Mississippi River delta performed exorcisms of the ponds. He came from an ancient line of shamans who'd freed blues players who sold their souls at crossroads. Self-proclaimed wizards sought to reverse the spell some evil spirit had cast over the Farm.

A Turëno shaman from Suriname brought his darts and blowgun, offering to kill whoever harmed the frogs. He showed anyone who wanted to see his secret vials of okopipi frog venom he had for that purpose. The shaman, "Dart Man," became a local celebrity for a few days until word of his offer leaked and rolled across social media.

The town's police chief urged him to take his pouch and return to Suriname. Enchanted youth protested but the shaman disappeared the next day.

A sorceress and teacher from the Tiger Striped Monkey Frog Clan of Ecuador offered to show locals how to heal themselves with moonfog dancing.

During the full moon, on a night when the fog was thin and translucent, barefoot dancers dressed in orange and black striped shirts, leapt and spun while they moaned guttural and high-pitched melodies supposed to replicate the din of thousands of frogs calling. Dancers of all ages thought it was great fun and volunteered to dance whenever the sorceress asked.

Local athletes jogged and yogis stretched. Kids gathered to watch the yoga and laugh as the old people practiced their slow, stiff versions of the 'frogger' exercises.

When the youngsters copied the elders, squatting, jumping, planking, crunching with frog spread legs at ten times faster than the old guard could manage, they heard, "Are you mocking us?"

"Can't we work out, too? This is fun."

"Lead on, grandpa," one of the kids said. "You rock!"

Numerous cases of depression were banished while

claims of asthma and arthritis healing flourished. Whispers of cures of lack of desire and shocking new experiences of passion circulated among the long-married.

Having heard that a colony of frogs was named 'an army,' squads of retired US Navy SEALs and US Marine Corps Special Forces and the National Guard showed up out of curiosity. The Seals offered to dive. Politely, James declined their offer due to shallow water and the danger to the untold numbers of active frogs and those hibernating in the mud.

When two of the ex-military volunteers wandered around town fully armed and belted with bullet sashes, the mayor called them and their commander to her office.

"Do not, I repeat, do not wear any guns or weapons in this town! This is not a war. We're a small peaceful town and you're scaring the hell out of our citizens! You have ten minutes to store your weapons in your vans. If I see any of you bearing arms! in my town! I will have you arrested!"

The military folks grumbled.

"We're just trying to help."

"We got the second amendment. She can't do anything."

"Hang on," an officer who didn't bring weapons called out to her colleagues. "We're dealing with a woman who kissed a frog in front of the whole world to save her little town," she said. "I wouldn't put it past her throwing you and us in jail and then suing."

One of the oldest vets said, "Hey, y'all. We're here to have some fun. Let's not spoil it."

The ex-military volunteers stowed their guns and ammunition. One left town. The others enjoyed a pleasant few weeks camping in townspeoples' back yards with their friends. They shared neighborhood barbecues and sat around firepits, sipping beer and telling war stories to fascinated audiences of kids and adults.

During that year, with encouragement from media attention, as embarrassing as it was, and the town's council offering tax breaks and free publicity, tourism flourished.

Developers erected new houses and refurbished aging ones. Vacant houses became rentals and a restaurant received a zoning change to build across the highway from the wetlands. Streets were paved. A new out-of-town bank branch appeared. The village grew to two thousand residents.

A few citizens became wealthy because a motel chain saw a future *Frogland* filled with rides and costumes to rival *Disney World*. They charged top dollars or euros or yen or yuan for the land close to the Farm.

By late spring of that year, both the volunteer and professional vernal poolers had birthed a new crop of tadpoles from the fertile ooze. At first sighting of the fishy-frogs, cheers went up and headlines flew out from the town's website.

Mr. Clemens, who liked the title his students gave him, "Frogologist in Chief," reminded everyone that tadpoles didn't mature to chirruping or croaking age for at least two years, more likely three. The excitement died down, but everyone kept their hopes high.

Digging a vernal pond with her neighbor, Rosa's abuela, the ageless Maria Elena, slipped and strained her back. Rosa took over and recruited her friend Aleema to help her build a pond large enough for thousands of tadpoles.

"Rosa, my sweet, I could love you to death for digging

up my yard," her grandma quipped.

"Don't say that, grandma. I don't want to die by hugging!"

Maria Elena laughed. "We'll raise coqui tadpoles. I know they'll sing. They're little mud angels."

Vernal poolers, who had become celebrities in the town and on the internet, released a hundred dozen three-year old tadpoles into the Farm ponds, hoping they were smart enough to avoid fish and large frogs long enough to grow to croaking age.

Those new tadpoles had spawned before the pond went silent. So, in high spirits and springtime optimism, the frog farmers and the townspeople gathered around the frog ponds listening.

No one heard a peep much less a trill or a croak. After a week, a shaman from the Amazon basin suggested an animal sacrifice.

"Yeah, we should kill an ox or something," said old man Bringle, the corner grocery store owner whose business had grown with the town. "I'll butcher it, smoke it for a few days. Mighty tasty."

"Nah, let's kill the frogs and eat 'em," practical residents said. Most of those were known curmudgeons or frail senior citizens outraged by the commercial frenzy in town.

"It's constant hammering and shouting everywhere in town."

"Worse than frog racket."

"There's so much traffic, I'm afraid to cross the street."

"It's time we were known for something besides frogs."

Neighbors who had never spoken up for fear of being embarrassed spoke up.

"My ears were tired of those frogs barking all the time."

"They might as well raise geese and donkeys."

"If I want to listen to chatter like that I can sit in on the Auxiliary meetings," said one old grump.

"I won't be able to afford the taxes," went a common complaint.

The holy people and retired military withdrew. The parting wisdom of the preachers was, "Wait and see. We're all in the hands of our Higher Power."

The shamans said, "The frogs are tired of their own voices. Let the spirits of the water repair their souls. They need peace and quiet to compose new music."

When they heard this metaphysical analysis broadcast on community TV, some of the locals objected. "Frogs don't have souls. Only people have souls!"

The shaman disagreed. "Perhaps it's not one frog with a soul, but all frogs together have a soul."

The only out-of-town spiritual leader who remained in town was a short, rotund woman from the state capital who claimed no powers or wisdom.

When asked why she'd joined the cavalcade of healers, she said, "I'm not a magician or a wise person. I'm just wondering ...."

Mornings and evenings she placed a cushion on the ground near a pond and sat with her eyes half-closed. A few locals brought their cushions and sat with the woman known as 'The Meditator.'

When asked how to do what she was doing, she said "Nothing."

A rumor spread that The Meditator and her clique could

hear voices within The Silence. This information piqued Rosa's inquisitive mind. She joined the group for their evening sits. She heard only a few splashes, birdcalls, and the breathing of other meditators.

One afternoon, while she and a couple of her friends, Fiona and Robbie, picnicked at the Reserve, Robbie said, "Look. Watch that one."

He pointed to a frog lounging on the bank, casting his tongue again and again into a swarm of gnats.

"Watch him swallow the bugs."

They gazed at the frog until Fiona said, "What?"

"Look at his eyes," Robbie said.

"How do you know it's a him?" Rosa asked, piqued at Rob's assumption.

"Her. It. Them. Just watch. Look at the eyes when they snatch a bug."

The frog flicked its tongue out and back. "Cool," Rosa said.

"Dope," Fiona said. "It's like they swallow their eyes when they gulp down the bug."

Robbie spread the word. Soon, frog observers showed up with binoculars to watch frogs' eyeballs suck back into their heads when they swallowed. Closeup videos showed lightning fast frog tongues snatching bugs followed by frog eyes flipping back down toward their throats.

After a few months, The Meditator left town, leaving behind a fellowship of pond sitters. Most mornings and evenings, they sat. Nobody paid much attention to them.

Until one day, one of the sitters noticed several frogs seeming to wave their legs as if trying to gain attention.

A frog sitting on a log would raise its front leg and flutter it for a moment. Across the pond another would lift its foot and clench its toes a few times. Later it would repeat the motion while another stretched its squat neck and swung it back and forth as if looking both ways before it crossed the pond.

When other frogs swam or hopped toward the waggling frogs and then they all disappeared into the brush or the muck, the meditators guessed that the waving frogs were male. They were sure the frogs had converted their mating calls into mating sign language.

When the coffee shop crew heard about the waving frogs, they spread the news. Most townspeople's reaction was to disregard the reports as self-induced visions.

James dispatched farmers to watch the pond around the clock. Volunteers from LFA, doubtful kids, and intrigued adults joined the farmers. Several observers spotted frogs waving and wiggling their legs and jutting their heads back and forth.

"Watch that one," a retired farmer said, pointing to a fat bullfrog at the far edge of Blue Boy Pond. "He's furling his toes like he's inviting another frog to join him!"

"The meditators were right!" the LFAers in the crowd said. "The frogs can communicate by signing! If they didn't, how would the girls know which guy they wanted?"

One LFAer swore he'd seen more than one frog doing pushups. "Like those lizards on TikTok," he said.

A studious farmer, hoping to find a way to keep the Farm going, discovered a similar ant phenomenon – some ants raise and lower their abdomens to signal food trails to other ants.

"Frogs are smarter than ants," he proclaimed.

Wits named the waving events "Frog Frolic Fluttering Frogs." Others preferred the name "Hula Frogs." Videos of the waving frogs went viral.

Theories abounded about the reasons for the motions. Fact finders learned about a frog living at the base of a waterfall in the Ecuadorian jungle. When the waterfall sounds crescendo in the spring, drowning out the frogs' calls, the males resorted to wiggling their legs like dancers.

According to the frog scientists, who didn't really know, the females chose their companions based on the power and beauty of a male's dance. When the waterfall's flow calmed down, males went back to singing.

A month after the first Frog Farm frog flutters, the frogs settled back into their normal torpor. The watchful LFA set up night and day vision cameras on every pond. During the course of the next month, a few frogs were filmed wiggling and waving.

None was seen doing pushups.

"We'll transmogrify"

As the months came and went, the town followed the advice of the learned and the holy to wait and let nature take its course.

A handful of culinarily curious residents who had never tasted frog netted and cooked them, substituting the frog meat in traditional chicken and fish recipes.

A cynical retelling of the frog princess myth circulated through some kitchens. A frog jumped into a princess's lap, asking her for a kiss. In exchange, he'd become a prince and she could be his wife and take care of him in the castle. She took him home, handed him over to her chef and, that evening, feasted on garlic-roasted frog legs in white wine and shallot sauce.

Regardless of boggy smells rising from the neighborhoods' ovens and skillets, the plucky residents forged ahead with their meals. These adventurous eaters named frog meat *The Chicken of the Swamps*.

Word got around that heavy frog eaters were feeling listless. Some retched and sweat and spent days inside their houses. Unable to discover a thick enough gravy to cover muddy taste no sauce could conquer, the cooks and their families called it quits.

Frog Frolic Farm business had tailed off. International competitors had spread the rumor that Frog Frolic frogs were radioactive. Few chefs believed it, but just in case ... they reduced their orders from Frog Frolic by more than half. A haze of dejection settled over the farmers and their families and friends. The town's economy dwindled as suddenly as it had risen.

Motel rooms and rental houses emptied out while the restaurants opened only three days every week. The bank kept a handful of tellers employed to show their faith in its customers and in nature. They allowed their mortgagees to pay late, if necessary, "... for at least another year," the bank president said.

"The banks don't have a choice," was the general opinion. A rumor flew around that a competing frog farm in the next state was hiring. Some of the frog farmers couldn't wait a year for normalcy so they and their families fled town for work.

Mrs. Gould, the ever-hopeful mayor, James, and the most conservative citizens stayed stalwart, wishing and praying, but beginning to see the end of a way of life.

Aleema and Marisol, Rosa's closest friends, would have to move a thousand miles away.

Hugging Rosa, Aleema said, "I already miss you."

"We'll facetime everyday," Rosa said, holding her friend.

Marisol looked into Rosa's misting brown eyes. "I'll miss you so much."

Rosa said, "You'll come back. I know it."

"I'll miss the froggies, too," Aleema said. "I liked their croaks and peeps."

"That's sad," Marisol said. "But I guess it doesn't matter anymore."

"We'll transmogrify," Rosa said, laughing, trying to add some humor to the sad departures. "We'll be some kind of crazy apart together thing," she added, a note of sorrow in her voice. They hugged each other and wept.

As they drove away, Rosa pledged to herself she'd immerse herself in her biology studies and make some new best friends.

The remaining frog farmers banded together, vowing to do everything they could to either bring back the frog voices or, at least, keep a small farm going.

"Frog farming's a good job," they said with pride. "Pays well. You need special skills. Besides, we're fighting climate change with our frogs. We feed bugs and worms, or the frogs catch flies and things. No carbon in our supply chain. Also, we have equal pay for equal work. We don't care where you came from, what you look like."

The frog farmers, once tucked away in the low end of the town's class structure, rose a few notches.

Life in the town settled down for the next year. Then, toward the end of the second anguished and silent summer, a young woman entrepreneur from the city arrived in town, knowing opportunity, innovation, and hard work could provide not only survival, but prosperity.

As it happened, James had met the woman (and developed a crush on her) at a culinary industry trade show the year before the frogs fell silent. She was a specialty foods marketer who had won awards for transforming failing food enterprises into thriving businesses.

While pondering his business choices, James found her business card in his desk drawer. Believing that chance was his best option, he immediately punched her number into his phone. She answered.

After a brief chat – she remembered him – he invited her to town to check out possibilities.

His Farm depended on ample consumption of frog meat. It didn't need singing or croaking frogs, but it did need a good reputation. And, as a fifth-generation frog farmer and town council member, he felt sympathy for his fellow citizens duty to them.

James told her, "If you can figure out how to help us, maybe we can hire you to come up a marketing campaign or something."

"Sounds like fun," she said.

She liked his Farm's name, needed a new challenge, and would commit to three months working for Frog Frolic Farm, if her assessment of the town's potential proved promising.

Queen of the Wetlands

Plagues

The scientists and the holy people had failed to break The Silence. Now, the townspeople were excited when they heard that James had hired a business expert.

He introduced her and her plan at the monthly Chamber of Commerce meeting. Her name was Calliope and she was named after the goddess of song.

"Call me Calli, not Ca-*lie*-oh-pea or *Cal*-e-ope," she told everyone, charming the Chamber members with her enthusiasm and vision. "People tell me I'm edgy and energetic," she said. She explained her dream for the town, rekindling the business people's enthusiasm.

The usual skeptics muttered their suspicions. For most, bubbles of the champagne of hope lifted their spirits.

When people first met her, they did call her Calli, but the four-note melody of her full name reminded them of the subtle frog harmonies they used to hear. They were a polite people, so most addressed her as "Ms. Cal-i-o-pea."

Her portrait and regular updates about her tourist ideas appeared on the Farm's and on the Chamber of Commerce websites. Some internet blogs and a couple of podcasts, persistent in their hunger for content no matter how irrelevant or tedious, posted random updates about the exciting prospects for the town.

Tweeters and bloggers found in the optimistic young woman's ideas and plans fodder for their mean and sometimes vicious attacks.

Calli was a bold entrepreneur who was invulnerable to caustic cracks in person or from the Internet's cast of heartless and brainless blathermouths.

High energy from the moment she woke up, ready to go to work, she understood how acceptance in the face of adversity could calm the mind and soul and trigger breakthrough ideas.

"I love meditating, and the pond sitters are onto something. But I can't sit more than three minutes," she confessed to the sitters and others. "My mind clears when I'm moving. Like when I stroll around the ponds or solve a big problem."

The mayor agreed. "Hear, hear," she said. "We have to *make something good happen*!"

In a speech to high school students, Calli said, "We have what's called a 'horned dilemma' – The Silence and the dragging economy. Let's fix 'em both!"

Loud cheers and stomping and chants rose up.

"Go, Calli!"

"Help the frogs!"

"Out, out, out with the old!"

" In, in, in with the new!"

"Out!"

"In!"

"Out!"

"In!"

Calli shouted back. "Keep learning. Read up on things. Tell me your ideas! I hear you have one of the best teachers of all time in this school. Work with him."

More pounding and cheering.

"Yay, Mr. Clemens!"

"Clemens, Clemens, he's our man."

"If he can't do it, nobody can!"

Kids erupted from the bleachers. A crowd gathered around Calli all wanting to share their ideas with her. Acrobats leapt and hopped, some doing handstands and back flips, others blasted music from their phones.

On her "Frogs for All" website and Facebook page, Calli cited an article from an obscure philosopher as an inspiration for an active kind of meditation everyone could do.

In a twentieth century book, *The Soul of Silence,* a philosopher proposed a solution to the spirit-shattering chaos of modern society. Humans should observe and imitate the normal silence of animals. He claimed the silence would heal spiritual and even physical maladies and bring peace to the wars between nations and resolve quarrels among peoples.

Calli titled her blog post "Listen like the frog" and urged her readers to accept the meaning of The Silence as a spur to change, not only frog things, but anything. The message appealed to the range of student cohorts and to most elders.

Continuing her work to unify the townspeople's focus and solidify their confidence in her plans, she composed "Frogs for All" theme song based on the old ballad "Sound of Silence." Calli kept the tune and changed the lyrics to "Hello, Silence, my old friend. All my sorrows you will mend."

Her fans said she had a genius for composing earworms.

She circulated ads on the internet and posted signs along all the new and old roads in and out of town. Calli displayed photos and drawings of frogs sitting blissfully on lily pads in bloom.

The advertising attracted fewer tourists than during the town's earlier growth spurt. However, as James the farmer and realist had expected, after visitors listened to nothing but bugs and birds and a few silent frogs, tourist traffic soon dried up.

Showing her intrepid spirit, Calli accepted the failure of her frog tourist venture. "Some things work, some don't," she told James. "Solving these big problems takes time."

James couldn't disagree. He encouraged her to come up with another plan. And, if she had the energy and the faith in herself and the town, come up with another, and another and another until she found a solution. "But remember, we have time, but we don't have infinite money."

"We have plenty, James." She smiled. "Don't worry."

Calli's charm and enthusiasm convinced James and everyone she spoke with to give her as many chances as she needed. She was fun, no matter if her plans worked or not.

The coffee club cronies agreed.

"If James wants to pay for her, we can play along."

"She's no expert."

"But she brings a good spirit."

"Yeah. Besides, she gives us stuff to talk about."

The weather, in the meantime, was misty and warm, a fine climate for amphibians. The silent frogs thrived. Invading squads were seen in yards, under porches, roosting in cisterns, huddling under hosta leaves, hunting moths, slugs, snails, and worms.

Nobody knew how the frogs had escaped the ponds. The leap-proof fences sunk into the soft soil around the Farm had contained them for decades. A few years back, Frog Frolic had tried electric fences with no luck.

Frog carcases littered the shores of the ponds. Frog Frolic ponds offered crows, buzzards, and flies a wild revel of nipping, pecking, and shredding.

The frogs became pests everywhere in town. Still, the

persevering residents were cautious and didn't try to remove or eliminate them.

"I don't mind one of them little tree frogs jumping into my car – one landed on my hand t'other day. Kinda cute," one of the seniors at the Senior Center told her bridge group. "But havin' them everywhere, good Lord!"

Drivers couldn't help but squash languid frogs lolling in the streets. Murders of crows and wakes of buzzards descended to feast on the remains splayed on the roads.

The seniors at the Senior Center claimed they recognized some of the crows from their venture the year before.

To the relief of the homeowners, a parliament of owls arrived at the same time a kettle of hawks began picking off the overfed, sluggish frogs when they emerged from hiding.

Within a week, the frog occupation of the town had ended. Owls lingered late into the morning near the Farm, and a small cast of red-tail hawks circled a few times every day. Crows malingered in the trees while turkey vultures circled in the sky hoping to scavenge any little corpse on the shores of the ponds.

Soon, the formerly free-hopping frogs, nature's role models for survival, kept to the densest corners of the bogs, hiding in the rushes and cattails.

One evening, during a stroll around Blue Boy pond, Calli noticed a horde of flies feasting on the decomposing carcass of a fish on the shore. As she watched, opportunistic frogs emerged from the water, snatching one fly after another before diving back under.

Her stick-to-itiveness, laudable if naïve, Calli dug into her creative brain. Never one to pass on an idea no matter how far-fetched, the next day she made a down payment on a herd of pigs, expecting them to attract flies to their paddock to nourish the frogs so well they'd sing their joy.

James liked what she did with pork in her kitchen but doubted the masses of flies would help crack The Silence.

"It's silly, Calli," he told her. "Loosing flies on the town is the dumbest thing I can imagine."

"I admit it's odd, but it's not silly. Besides, we're keeping your frog farmers employed. A new venture is what this town needs to keep its spirits up."

James shook his head but said he'd wait and see for a couple of weeks. He reminded her again that Frog Frolic had tried feeding the frogs a cornucopia of flies early on in The Silence.

"We tried feeding them super frog food – flies, slugs, minnows. The whole pantry. It didn't work," James said. "Besides, flies? Nobody will put up with it. Flies spread disease. They thrive in shit. And hogs stink!"

"I know it's outrageous," Calli said. "It's just one small idea. Give it a shot."

Against his better judgment, but following his heart's openness to Calli, James built a barn and paddock on the Farm, housed and fed the pigs.

At first, the farmers objected to "hog farming" as the pigs attracted throngs of flies. She calmed the farmers and the other citizens with her confidence and prediction that swarms of flies would stay near the ponds nourishing the frogs, healing their vocal cords or whatever their problem was.

"Don't worry," Callie pronounced. "Flies mean we're on our way to success."

The townsfolk believed enough in "Crazy Calli" that their hopes rose with every buzz, expecting the frogs' natural response would be to indulge in flies and, sooner or later, start to croak.

At the coffee shop, retirees all agreed the trade-off between smelling foul hog odors for a short time and enjoying frog songs would be worth it. The town's optimists agreed.

"Gotta try new things."

"Get outta the rut."

"If it works, she'll be a hero."

"We'll all be heroes."

Football fanatics said to their fellow coffee drinkers, "You don't score unless you can change it up at the line of scrimmage!"

The town overcame its common sense, falling into line with Callie's wishful thinking.

The frogs devoured the bonanza of flies but their appetites couldn't keep up with the escalating profusion of bugs of all kinds.

The fly occupation spread from the hog yards to everywhere in town.

Trees and lawns filled with the din and waste of flocks of hungry starlings while opportunistic hordes of grackles darkened the sky over the hog pens.

Soon, those who went outside wore wide-brimmed hats, mosquito nets and ear protectors. A few of the most sensitive citizens closed their houses and fled.

From the satiated frogs – not a peep.

Graced with charismatic self-confidence and never without at radical idea, Calli found a quick answer to the fly riot.

First, she bought thousands bags of fly parasites from a bug ranch in Colorado. The tiny insects, branded as "Fly Wranglers," burrowed into fly eggs and feasted on the larvae before they could hatch into repulsive adult flies.

Calli dusted her hog yards with the parasites and gave the rest of the bags away to anyone who wanted them. The "Fly Wranglers" stalled the flourishing of the flies for a few days, giving the townsfolk a respite from the buzzing infestation.

The crafty flies, hidden in the nooks and crannies in yards, garages, houses, laid eggs and produced new swarms.

Resolute in her belief in pig power to save the town from The Silence, Calli invested in enough bug zappers for every house and building and yard.

Crackles and *tsssts* of singed flies, gnats, mosquitoes, even grasshoppers and nameless other bugs sizzled throughout the days and nights and cut the fly population to tolerable levels.

Undaunted by the flies, Calli tried to postpone the inevitable loss of her hog business using road signs in flashing neon to advertise. The signs and her website scrolled images of clean photogenic swine and piglets dancing on the town common and catching apples tossed by a diversity of people of all ages.

Calli updated her social pages daily with new pictures of pigs. She tweeted a storm and posted thousands of Facebook pictures and Instagram invitations.

Her various social accounts rocketed in a few days to more than 100,000 followers.

Unfortunately for all concerned, the signs and ads and social media didn't help. Happy pigs in real life couldn't compete with singing pigs on TV, so even the few tourist children were disappointed.

The flies adjusted their birth rates to the pre-zapper days and the fly population swelled to new peaks. They attracted what seemed like millions more starlings that colonized the trees, dripping waste on lawns, cars, houses. Walkers stayed far away from overhanging branches.

Angry citizens felt disgusted and misled.

"It's just like those cannabis people."

"We approved one store, then we had seven."

"She promised a few flies. She gave us a few trillion!"

A squad of frog farmers pulled out their trusty shotguns offering to help anyone who wanted to dispose of the filthy birds in the trees.

The sheriff ignored the armed men as they patrolled the tree-lined streets, aiming their weapons into the tree canopies.

The crashing sound of the shotguns reverberated through the afternoons as countless dead birds rained down. Kids on their bikes followed the starling hunters ahead of the town's bucket loaders and garbage trucks.

The mayor scheduled a special meeting of the town council to request that Calli drop the hog business or, at least, scale it back.

Ignoring signs of a growing incursion of rats and mice, and day-long wakes of vultures darkening the sky, the town council was unified on one measure: Business was good for the town, even if it was gross.

"Can't please everybody all the time," they said.

Simi Donata, the town clerk and part-time preacher of The Church of the Violet Flame of St. Germaine, rose from her chair and asked for the microphone.

When the audience quieted, she said, "Honorable mayor, elected counselors, friends, fellow citizens. I'm here to speak for the silent minority."

As Simi walked to the front of the room, light clapping sounded from around the room.

"Madame Mayor, many of us believe ...," she paused,

turned and raised her free arm toward the audience as if embracing them, "our town is cursed. We need a miracle."

Half the counselors dropped their jaws. Silence lasted a few seconds until a chorus of voices arose, some in complaint, some cheering, some laughing.

"Hear hear!"

"We don't believe in curses."

"That's medieval."

"Miracles are superstition."

"Simi speaks."

"We already had an exorcism."

"It was bogus!"

"Miracles are real! I've witnessed three!"

"Tell us, Simi."

When the crowd settled, Simi faced her neighbors.

"First we had a plague of frogs. And I don't mean The Silence."

"That's right. I squished about a thousand with my car."

"I found three in my kitchen sink!"

"My dog puked he ate so many!"

"I have to keep my kids inside."

"Yeah, they have to shower when they come in."

All five counselors nodded their heads in agreement.

Simi lowered her voice, speaking contralto into the microphone. "Then we had a plague of flies!"

"We still have it!"

"They drove my neighbors out of town!"

"I'll never get all the fly specks off my siding."

"You all agree. I can tell. It's a plague," Simi said. "The gods are talking. They talk with nature's voice."

"It's a plague," some of her congregants repeated, as if following Simi's call and response preaching. "Flies and maggots!"

"Flies and maggots!"

"What about the birds?" someone in the back row hollered.

"It's raining freakin' birdshit!"

"The gods are talking shit!"

Laughter erupted with some people nearly falling off their chairs.

The eighth-grade history teacher chimed in. "We love birds, but we hate starling shit."

"Somebody should collect it and sell it as guano!"

"My roses are blooming like crazy. They love it."

Clapping and foot stomping and whistling broke out. The mayor looked over at Calli where she sat with James on the aisle near the back exit. Mrs. Gould wondered if Calli would leave to escape abuse the citizens' pent-up anger could lead to.

Isaiah, the longest serving counselor, the town butcher, the most conservative counselor, and the only person in the hall wearing a suit and tie, waved at everyone, and yelled as loud as he could. "Quiet in the peanut gallery!"

Shou Lan, his liberal archrival stood beside him. She raised a sign. It read, Respect.

Most of the audience stopped shouting and speaking.

"You know, people. This is not politics," Isaiah said.

"It's worse than politics."

Almost everyone laughed.

Shiou Lin nodded to Simi, "What is it, Preacher Donata?"

saying with sincere curiosity in her voice.

Everyone waited, knowing the answer.

Simi looked around the room, her forehead wrinkled, shaking her head back and forth and up and down.

"We all know what it is." She pointed to the audience.

"It's a plague," a dozen voices called.

"Yes. It is," Simi said, deepening her frown. "It's another plague. A plague of birds!" She heaved a sigh and her shoulders sank. She crossed the room in front of the counselors' table. Her long gown, the yellow and violet colors of St. Germaine, dragged behind her as if it were a queen's mantle. "I'm afraid it's biblical. We'll see more plagues before we know it."

"I don't believe that," a small gray-haired woman with a smoker's gravelly voice spoke above the din. "It's on account of the hog sh ... manure."

"What can we do? What shall we do?" Myralee, the teacher, asked.

One of the St. Germaine congregants clapped her hands and yelled, "I know! I know!"

No one paid attention to her until Simi raised her voice.

"Rhonda. Tell us. What do you know?"

"We need a miracle. We need a Moses!"

A ruckus developed as the crowd gabbled and joked.

Bronson, the youngest frog farmer, raised her hand and waved. Sitting next to her, Troung, her best friend climbed up on his chair and shouted, "Listen up! She knows what she's talking about."

Noise continued.

Mrs. Gould tapped her gavel gently at first, then louder,

as she called out "Bronson, go ahead!"

The mayor hammered the gavel until the crowd calmed down. "All right, Bronson. Thank you for your politeness. What do you have to say?"

Clearing her throat, looking down, shy Bronson squeaked, "It's not a curse."

"What's that?"

"Can't hear you."

"Speak up, young one."

Bronson tried again. "It's not a curse. It's not a plague. It's a problem is all. It's just the frogs need a break and everybody's overreacting!"

She collapsed onto her seat, her head bowed as she listened to the quiet.

From the back, Mr. Clemens commented, "Nice work, Bronson. You're practicing your critical thinking."

After a moment while the audience discussed Bronson's opinion, with a tight smile, Mrs. Gould said, "All right, folks. Control yourselves. This is your meeting. It'll go better if you follow the rules. Please try."

"Why should we?"

"Everything else is out of control!"

Surprised by the surly rebuke of the mayor, the room went quiet.

Simi spoke into an embarrassed silence.

"We're a small town. There's no doubt we're cursed. We need help. We're in huge trouble with the spirits of the wild. St. Germaine can help, but we gotta ask her."

Bronson, feeling stronger now that people listened to her, called out. "I agree. But it's not a curse!"

Rhonda shouted, "We need a miracle!"

"It's not a curse," Bronson said. "We didn't do anything wrong. We've done everything right. The best we could."

Commotion again, until Calli stood up. She waited until the counsel looked her way and Mrs. Gould tapped the gavel until the only sound in the room came from the ceiling fans.

A sharp voice called out. "You're no Moses."

"She's the pharaoh. She caused this!"

"Yeah. She brought the hogs right into town."

"It's her right. She owns the property."

"Yeah, well, she's new in town. We solve our own problems."

Calli waited, frowning and nodding.

"You're right. I'm no Moses," she said.

"That's for sure."

"You're a fraud."

Squabbling and arguing resumed.

"She's doing her best!"

"It's not good enough!"

"Blame her, not the spirits!"

"She raised the spirits with all the damn hogs!"

Mrs. Gould rose and pounded the gavel in a rhythm.

Babum babum babum bumbum.

She smiled as the counselors followed her with their palms beating **Babum babum babum bumbum** on the tabletop.

First a chuckle, then sparse sniggering, then a gentle laughter as the tension dropped and everyone turned to look at Calli.

"I'm no Moses," she said. "And I am to blame."

"That's right."

Surprise showed on many faces.

"Go on, Calli," Mrs. Gould said.

Calli continued. "I'm at least part of the problem. I tried to help the frogs and the town but all I did was cause a big mess."

"That's for sure," angry citizens muttered.

"I'm sorry. I apologize to all of you. I kept my hog farm as clean as possible. It even won an award from the Future Farmers for my sanitation program. But still, my hog farm was a failure."

"Worse than that."

Confused grumbling like background static in the room.

"At least she said she was sorry."

"So what?"

"My porch screens are clogged with fly crap!"

Mrs. Gould tapped a few mild beats. "Give her a chance, folks. She has something to tell us."

"It better be good."

"You can't stop the plague unless we get a miracle," Rhonda said followed by loud clapping from her close friends.

"As of now," Calli said, her voice stern, "I'm closing down the hog farm. I'll ship them out and clean up the lots."

"When? How can we believe you?" Simi asked.

"I promise," Calli said. "I'll make the promise on my website and my social and document the shipment and the cleanup on video, if you want."

A universal shaking of heads.

"We'll believe it when we see it."

"But what if the flies and the birds don't leave?"

"Yeah, they like it here."

Bronson faced Callie. "Sorry, Calli. Sorry, Mr. Clemens. You can't get rid of them overnight. It's natural selection."

Calli turned to Mr. Clemens.

Reluctant to abuse his authority, she rose anyway. "Bronson is right. There's a natural process involved here. And just so you know, I consider nature itself a miracle."

His students in the audience clapped, as did several adults.

"Here's what will probably happen," Mr. Clemens said. "Calli will clean out the hogs and their manure. The birds and the frogs will devour the flies over a few days or weeks. Then, we'll be back to normal."

"Let's hope so," Rhonda said. "That would be a miracle."

Isaiah stood up. "I'm your counselor," he proclaimed. "And even better, I'm your butcher. I have a good idea for Calli – what she can do with her hogs." He put his hand on his chest and paused.

"Whaaat?"

"Out with it, Isaiah."

A regular council opponent said from the front row. "If it's any good, you got my vote next time."

A few people chortled.

"I'll buy them. Every hog." He raised his eyebrows as he addressed Callie, "If she gives me a good price ...."

"Make an offer," Calli said, grinning. "Not only that, anything you pay I'll use for a fly and bird cleanup fund."

"We accept," a wag volunteered for everyone."

Calli raised her finger. "After cleanup expense, that is...."

"Whatever."

"That's fair."

Noah stood up next to Isaiah. "Here's another idea. If Isaiah agrees, let's have a town party with those hogs. Everybody can contribute what they want and we'll give the money to the fund."

"Yo. You're the drip," the LFA representative called.

"That's why you guys are our counselors."

"Good ideas."

More hubbub in the room.

Noah raised his arms over his head and clapped. Mrs. Gould lightly tapped her tabletop rhythm again.

When the crowd quieted, Noah turned to Isaiah and said, "We'll give the money to the fund ... after buying and butchering expenses, of course."

Laughter rang out.

"Bring on them ribs."

"Make mine pork chops!"

"It'll be a hambone party!"

"I love pork tenderloins!"

General laughter and even a few hugs circulated. Simi took Rhonda by the arm and strolled over to Calli.

Simi said, "You were the agent of the spirits. You brought their curse. But they're forgiving. Maybe you can be the agent of their miracle."

"Thank you, Simi. I try my best every day," Calli said. "Sometimes I screw up. Today you all helped me. Next time I'll get it right."

"Oh, no," Rhonda groaned, whispering to Simi. "If she does something else, she'll bring another plague."

Simi nodded toward Calli. "Let's give her one more chance."

Simi and Calli shook hands while Rhonda glowered.

Mr. Clemens, sensing the teachable moment, clambered up on his chair.

"People. Folks. Everybody. Please. Before you leave." His current and former students stopped and waited. "Calli messed up. She flubbed. She made a miscalculation."

"We like your big words, Mr. Clemens," a graduate said.

Tittering in the room.

"Calli screwed up," Mr. Clemens said. "But here are today's three lessons. First, talking together we found a solution. Second, don't be afraid of failure. Trial and error, new idea, try again. Fail. Try again. It's how we grow. Third, we're gonna have a good ole time at our barbecue!"

Everyone clapped then rose and started for the door.

Playing his essential role as the town's favorite curmudgeon and coffee club founder, Willie Viella raised his voice. "It ain't over, folks. It ain't over till the birdshit and the flyspecks disappear. Then we can have a party."

"We'll see," Isaiah reminded everyone. "We'll wait and see."

The next morning, Calli and Isaiah arrived at a price both thought fair and beneficial to the town. She had the hogs delivered to the pens behind his shop. She and her crew shoveled out and spread lime and plowed it in across her swine lots.

Always an opportunist and pleased about how the hogs had fertilized the lots, she planted some of them with blueberry bushes and others with heirloom peaches.

Within a month, the inundations subsided. The townspeople, relieved, pleased that they'd been heard, relaxed into The Silence.

"Better no frog singing than bugs up our noses."

"The mayor shouldn'a let that woman bring in so many hogs."

"I'm gonna send her a bill for five-hundred dollars to clean up my yard!"

"Me, too."

Later, at the high school, Mr. Clemens used the onslaught of flies and birds as a biology lesson.

"That was a heck of a lesson in natural selection, the way the flies adjusted their reproduction," Mr. Clemens told his students as they washed fly specks off the wall of the school's maintenance shed.

Rosa spoke up in class. "What I liked was we had a real-life example of unintended consequences."

"Yeah, like how them hogs stank," Rain said, pinching her nose.

"I musta shot ten thousand of them damn birds. It was fun," Augie piped up.

"Watching those flocks of swallows and swifts swooping satisfied my soul," the class poet pined.

"Oh my god. That's sick."

"I was getting used to listening to the birds chirping. Sounded almost like peepers squalling."

"It wasn't all bad."

"No. Just ninety-nine point ninety-nine percent of the time!"

The mayor announced a date for the barbecue. She told her constituents that the popular bar band, "Swamp Holler," would play for the party and "Scoopy Dew," the local ice cream parlor, would supply all the ice cream anybody could eat.

Another Calli idea

The hogs and flies departed.

On a sunset walk around the ponds, James told Calli, "I don't want to say . . . I won't say it."

"Yeah, I know. It was stupid," Calli said, repentant. "But! We can't let a little screw-up stop us."

"Okay," James said, chuckling, shaking his head in wonder at Calli's indomitable spirit. "What's your next idea."

"It's much better," she said. "You'll love it."

James couldn't resist. He was feeling a little desperate and more vulnerable to her charms every day.

Ever the entrepreneur, and with James's financial support, Calli proposed a research project of scientists from the state university.

They could come up with a bio-tech solution. The college biology department agreed to try.

Cautioning Calli, James said. "We already gambled on experts. No luck at that table."

"James, we can't give up. The experts you had were old school. Let's go for a futuristic solution. Ways you and I and everybody else in town have no ideas of."

James forwarded scholarship funds for three biology students to set to work.

When word got around, the idea excited Rosa and the LFA. When Rosa tried to join the team of college students on the project, they told her she'd be in the way.

"Come back when you understand science," they said. "We have work to do."

Fuming, Rosa told Mr. Clemens, hoping he could influence the college students.

"Sorry, Rosa. You know they won't let you in on their hoity-toity research. They're trying to build their reputations. They think you'll distract them from their original research."

"I help them," Rosa protested. "You know that."

"You'll get your chance when the time is right," Mr. Clemens said. "Besides, from what I hear, you probably know more biology than they do."

Still furious, Rosa wrote emails to the college biology department, letters to the administration, made calls to town kids at the school, begging them to help. She knew if she could get her hands on the equipment in the college labs, she'd learn something important. None of her entreaties helped.

She met with James, offering to join the study for free. He shrugged.

"I'm sorry, Rosa. I could make a phone call, but it won't do much good," he said.

"Could you ask Ms. Calli?" Rosa asked.

"Sorry again. We agreed with those darn college bureaucrats it was to be their project. Once they got started, we aren't supposed to interfere."

Rosa stomped out of James's office, angry and hurt.

After a few weeks, Rosa's hurt subsided. In her mind, she scorned the college kids. She dug into the research she'd done over the years on her own. Maybe she'd discover the new species, maybe she'd finally pin down why the frogs went silent. What she really wanted to know was how the frogs communicated in silence.

During the months of university research, while everyone in town waited for the results, Calli and James got to know each other. Theirs was a slow-burning romance – she had a lot on her mind and little time for a relationship – but he persisted. They became a familiar couple around town.

Pelophylax esculentes

During the research lull, the multi-talented Calli wrote an environmental thriller titled *The Silence of the Frogs*.

With the title reminiscent of the famous movie, *The Silence of the Lamb*, she banked on the enormous amount of publicity the silent frogs had received and the followers she'd gained.

Calli's novel became a best seller. One of the subplots was set in a Bronze Age tribe of frog farmers. Their technology was almost the same as Frog Frolic Farm's.

With her book earnings and a TubeTV contract, Calli bought and settled into one of the town's preeminent homes, a Victorian house with four floors and three towers.

Calli intuited it was the American traditional recipes for frog cuisine that turned out tough, stringy, inedible meals during the town's foolhardy weeks of frog gorging. She decided to go back to the source of frog cookery. She enrolled in on-line French cooking classes to learn about which frogs to cook and which to leave alone.

She found the common name – "edible mud frogs" – for the everyday culinary frogs disgusting. Their scientific name, *Pelophylax esculentes*, sounded exotic and tasty. Calli began work on her next volume, a cookbook titled *Calli Does It! Exotic Asian Cuisine*.

James and his Farm team supplied her with a boundless supply of raw ingredients. She developed appetizers, entrees, sides, and desserts that tasted subtly like algae, but no more earthy than popular seaweeds and farmed tilapia.

One of her favorite parts of the cookbook was its collection of international myths and tales about frog princes and brides and queens. The high school art class provided funny and profound drawings and paintings.

Her cookbook began, "Amphibians are sacred. When we eat them, we are taking the transformative soul of the earth into our bodies."

The cookbook didn't sell well outside the region. Besides, Calli's restless nature found writing too solitary and she hated sitting. She decided to take her recipes to the town and open a restaurant.

When she told James of her latest brainstorm, she said the best way to "power up the Frog Frolic brand" was to start a restaurant. She argued that a successful upscale eating place serving delicious meals of frog foods would be the quickest way to restore the Farm's reputation and expand the market.

"It's going to be a lot of work and take some time," she said.

"But look what happened with tofu. It was just weird soy curds and now it's everywhere."

James grinned when he heard her latest pitch. He teased, "If you can cook frog as well as you can sell your ideas, we might make some money."

The bank agreed to lend her funds and James would help her with a down payment, if she needed. She could pay it back if the restaurant succeeded.

"When. Not if," Callie said, poking James in the shoulder.

Canny entrepreneur that she was, Calli surveyed the townsfolk for their favorite recipes. She then transformed them into gourmet frog dishes, naming specials of the day after cooks who supplied the original recipes.

Soon new signs sprouted around the town and a *Chez Calliope* Facebook page popped up.

Chez Calliope
Down Home Fusion Cooking

Curious about Calli's changes to their recipes and flattered to have specials named after them, the home cooks brought their whole families to the restaurant and became regular customers.

Her menus went viral, social media roiled with more jokes and recipe ideas, and her reputation soared.

Before long, customers were forced to make reservations a week in advance for the life-changing experience of devouring amphibian meals.

The restaurant's basic menu offered frog filet, frog lasagna, frog burgers, frog spaghetti, baked frog au vin, chicken-fried frog leg nuggets, and vegetables accompanied by frog fries.

The restaurant's most popular dish was Deep Fried Louisiana Frog Legs.

Customers left praise on the website and circulated them on their media.

"Try the Crawdaddy Nuggets. Better than chicken."

"They're sorta like chewy French fries."

"Dip 'em in cocktail sauce and you'd think they were fresh- water lobsters."

"Her FroGumbo can't be beat!"

The restaurant's oddest, and least popular, recipe was Calli's Twitchy Miso Soup. Since skinned frogs' legs don't firm up for hours after the frogs die, the fresh legs trembled and twitched in hot salty soup.

While most of the town turned down the chance to eat frog legs wiggling in their soup, grandfathers took their grandkids out for a rite of passage meal at *Chez Calliope*.

Few children would eat the soup. "Eeewww . . . gross," they said, squirming in their chairs. "They look like worms."

The grandfathers chuckled. "You gotta try new things. How else will you learn?"

The old fellas usually had to finish their grandchildren's frog meals. Or, as most did, leave the limp legs quivering in the bowls.

The restaurant's kitchen creativity soared. *Chez Calliope's sous chef*, an ex-frog farmer, invented high-protein frog chips. Nobody could just eat one.

Exotic combinations with multiple iterations of sauces with frog required regular menu changes. On the Asian section of the menu, Frogs Legs with Grains of Huanjia spice, orange rind and spring onions became popular with daring diners.

For dessert, customers ordered baked, chilled, or frozen frog desserts. The common opinion was "Calli's desserts are *almost* as good as homemade with normal ingredients."

Soon enough, kitchen work and restaurant management became routine for Calli's restless soul. She turned her imaginative and analytical mind to direct solutions of the frog silence problem.

With her urging, James sent eggs, tadpoles, and infant frogs to the famous Frog Research Facility in Manaus, Brazil, in hopes the PhD's would discover a biological source of the silence.

Like Dr. Yvette, they found nothing unusual about the frog voice boxes. In fact, once the infant frogs from Frog Frolic grew up in the Amazonian climate, they chirped and croaked like normal frogs.

When James heard this, he told his crew, half-joking, "No worries. We might have to wait a few years till our weather warms up enough, but we'll be raising singing frogs in our own jungle."

Closings

During the year of her serving diners' pleasures with amphibian gourmet at *Chez Calliope*, Calli imported living, croaking frogs to raise in restaurant aquariums.

They appealed to curious newcomers and to regulars who came in to listen and feel nostalgic.

Due to the restaurant's overwhelming success and demand for frogs, the Farm's edible population shrank to precarious levels. Calli reduced her orders from Frog Frolic and imported frogs from out-of-state and overseas. They were small, but her chefs made them tasty.

A little remorseful, Calli instructed her team to introduce a hundred dozen of the latest imports to the ponds with hopes of quickening frog songs.

"It might work," she said. "With fewer adult frogs now, nature might heal real fast. Worst case, we'll know in a couple of years when these new frogs produce full grown tadpoles."

Calli, an ethical entrepreneur, now a tired one, prepared

other amphibian dishes with little success among her customers. She also concocted selections of turtle soups. Only the most gourmand frog food patrons enjoyed turtle enough to order the soups more than once.

Exhausted as she'd never been before, Calli shut down her restaurant, gave all her employees a big bonus, and went home to recover from the restaurant demands.

A business realist, she calculated that her savings and the earnings from her book and TV deals would hold her over until she finished the sequel to her best-selling thriller.

When *Chez Calliope* closed, James decided to sell the Farm's remaining frogs. But every frog farm from Louisiana to France to Thailand was on red alert. Fearing infection worse than silence, none would buy.

The uncertainty surrounding the Frog Frolic Farm's silent frogs forced every frog farm in the world to be vigilant for any signs of fading frog cries.

A rumor had spread among the international frog chefs that a gene for silence and eventual death of all frogs had been loosed on the world not from Frog Frolic, but from a remote swamp in the Philippines.

The fear was irrational, the claim unfounded, like every conspiracy theory. Silent frogs at the Farm reproduced, thrived, and were as tasty as the noisy ones.

Instead of contagious frog silence around the world, a wild frog hunting frenzy erupted in isolated wetlands. Almost all the frogs trapped and offered to chefs in the cities were too small.

In time, when they couldn't find reliable markets

to sell their contraband, all but the most desperate or traditional frog hunters gave up. Peace returned to the backwaters.

James sold the nets and closed the sluices, shut down the abattoir, sold his trucks, and laid off the last frog farmers and snake and bird routers. The townsfolk were not surprised. They'd expected the demise of the Farm ever since the frogs stopped calling.

Before long, Frog Frolic Farm slipped back into its original wild bogginess.

Cattails thrived now they were no longer trimmed, algae flourished, and growing flocks of redwing blackbirds nested marshside. Swifts and swallows commanded the evening air over the ponds.

James and Calli made plans to move on.

She thought they might start an oyster mushroom or shiitake business.

James teased her. “Let's be bold. We could grow magic mushrooms for medicine!”

Thousands of James's frogs ended up as experiments in university labs. Uncountable tadpoles and frogs stayed down on the Farm, in the ponds.

When they weren't dozing, tongue-flicking, snacking, swimming, mating, or hibernating, the frogs found safe places in the shallows and sat, watching, waiting.

Frog Frolic Reserve

With some of her savings, Calli bought half of the frog Farm from James. Then they donated the property to their mutual creation: The Frog Frolic Reserve Trust. They incorporated the Trust with the covenant that no frog farming could ever happen there again.

James ran the Reserve for a while, happy to oversee the demolition of all farm buildings but the maintenance shop. He supervised the scientific tests and cultural events before he and Calli settled on the next venture. He transferred the Farm's pond management data to the Reserve. It included years of reports on air and water temperature fluctuations, rainfall, stream flow control, pond depth levels, pH readings, estimated annual frog populations by species, antibiotic use, and enormous amounts of other information.

Outside researchers had to meet the Frog Frolic Reserve's stringent rules. They were not permitted to net frogs or dig them up from the mud. They were encouraged to wait at the sloughy edges of the ponds then catch them with their hands.

A corps of kids volunteered to teach researchers how to pick up and hold a frog once it allowed itself to be enfolded by caring fingers.

As the pond rose, kids and young grown-up kids bragged about how they'd dived into the deepest spots and held their breath as long as they could. The record was two minutes twelve seconds.

The more adventurous swam underwater through the waterweeds. They found clumps of frog eggs clustered on the dangling roots of lily pads. Some would take waterproof phones or cameras down with them to take pictures of the dense, diaphanous bubbles to prove their claims.

As time passed, townspeople held out new hope that, given time, Mother Nature would bring back song from the amphibian wilderness.

Ever mindful of their purpose – to maintain an environment where frogs would sing and flourish – and aware of the needs of the researchers, volunteers organized a crew of algae scoopers. They called themselves "The Pond Scum Gang."

SOF protested the name. "Algae isn't scum. It's not a plant. Not an animal. It's an alien being," they joked.

The elders said, "Alien? What do you mean? Don't be silly."

"Algae's not really alien," Carmela told them. "Algae is a protist."

"Protist?"

"Sounds like 'protest,' right?"

The elders smiled.

"Before you get started, I'll ask Mr. Clemens to give you a seminar on algae. It will blow your minds."

One of the most important and arduous jobs for the Gang was to stir the water gently to prevent algae's frog-choking eutrophication. Careful to leave leaf and branch sediment undisturbed so the gooey sludge wouldn't release methane, volunteers heaped excess algae onto piles on the shores. They bagged it for selling to the gardeners in town. The proceeds went to the fund the Reserve's upkeep.

Some of the algae sales went to fight the illegal importation and cultivations of exotic amphibians, especially transparent frogs, psychedelic toads, and whistling salamanders.

The Gang's other critical job was the elimination of duckweed, the prolific plant that floated on the surface of warm, still water.

Dense duckweed absorbed so much oxygen the tadpoles beneath them would gasp and choke. At the same time, duckweed protected frogs, disguising them in the shallowest water while they hunted mites and spiders and bees.

The Gang formed a special squad of "Duckweedies" or "Weedies" who balanced the nutritional needs of the Reserve's tadpoles and adult frogs.

An imaginative Weedy, Rosa knew most of the natural world could help humans, even the most dangerous like poisonous recluse spiders, copperhead snakes, alligators. She decided to research duckweed to learn if it had any use at all.

What she learned astonished her. Besides food for ducks and shelter for frogs during spawning, in the right amounts it could oxygenate the water. Some people ate duckweed in their salads. Three of Rosa's friends who lived near the ponds wanted to grow duckweed, dry it, and sell it for human and animal food. They claimed it had more protein per ounce than cows' milk. They knew of a company that was commercializing algae for food.

As a group, even if it was a tempting idea, the Pond Scum Gang decided the Reserve ponds were too small to raise duckweed for food. Besides their mission was to help cultivate the ponds for human and all kinds of animals' pleasure.

That meant controlling duckweed, algae, cattails, the land-hungry knotweed, and any other plant that could threaten the pond life and beauty of the Reserve.

The Weedies learned to manage the sluices so the right amount of water circulated duckweed so it wouldn't overwhelm the frogs' and tadpoles' algae feed.

Pond maintenance became a critical and noble job for volunteers. At low water, multi-colored carpets of algae sometimes a quarter-inch thick could lay on the ponds. Daring fox and bobcat kits could tip-toe across the algae as they crept up on frogs lazing in the sun.

On the shores, knotweed charged toward the water like an army armored with poles and blades. Along some of the ponds, an eight-foot-tall hedge could overwhelm the walking path.

At the monthly meeting, one of the Weedies proposed letting the knotweed grow, then harvesting it for bioplastic.

"That's a stupid ...." his partner began. A current of groans and headshaking rippled across the group.

"You want to smother the ponds?"

"We do that, we kill everything, frogs, birds, toads.

Everything."

"That would be the apocalypse for the salamanders and the bass."

The Reserve's paid farmers cropped the knotweed stalks, dug up the roots, and spread ashes over the obstinate leafy towers. It took three years to control the knotweed bushes, then required dogged year-round attention from determined knotweed choppers and diggers.

Rosa, a natural diplomat, thanked the farmers as they slashed and burned the knotweed.

"You guys remind me of pioneers clearing the land," she said. "Remember to allow reeds and cattails to grow along the edges."

Since the Farm's transformation into a Reserve, and without regular attention from the formerly large crew of Frog Frolic farmers, cattails decided they owned ponds, spreading out from the edges of the ponds.

Hearing Rosa's gentle request, one of the older, louder Weedies piped up.

"Yeah, we gotta let the lady frogs have a safe place to lay their eggs," they said.

"No worries," the former farmers said. "It hasn't been that long since we farmed for a living."

For the love of the pond and feelings of civic

duty to the town, farmers brought out their tools and set to work with the volunteers. They hacked and chopped the cattails back, leaving wide swaths alone for their beauty and the frogs' ease.

Some townspeople and volunteer docents worked all day, all week to protect the frogs from poachers and avian and animal troublemakers. Soon, the frog population began to recover from *Chez Calliope's* depredations. The Reserve hoped a full return soon to a thriving frog population.

One of the enterprising docents opened Frogtown Arts, a cooperative art gallery where local painters and photographers displayed their works portraying scenes from the reserve.

A few of the artists sold their work online. Most were happy to invite their friends and families to openings and share their seasonal perspectives on the wild ponds.

One of the photographers was a would-be impresario. He sponsored monthly events at the musty old museum while looking for sponsors to help him rehabilitate the building and revive the displays.

Looking for tasks to keep volunteers busy, the Gang started a Sluicers squad. Their job was to protect the frogs from flood or droughts caused by erratic weather. They would raise the sluice gates after storms, closing them to managing meager inflows when rainless months could drop the ponds' volumes to dangerous levels.

The Sluicers' motto was: "All life is water. Everything else is weather."

BOOK II

THE SCIENTIST'S INSTINCT

The S Prize

Spec Ops for Frogs

Curious high-school kids played with the algae in the school labs. They found it could produce biofuel from its oil and, as it grew, it drew carbon dioxide out of the air.

During the high school chemistry class's review of the Periodic Table that year, Mrs. Hetzel, the chemistry teacher, organized her students into Table of Elements teams. Their goal was to understand the elements by focusing on the effects of atmospheric carbon and nitrogen reduction and the commercial possibility of biofuels.

When Rosa learned that hydrogen could be produced from algae, she lobbied the Pond Scum Gang to contact some company to take all the algae they needed. The Gang was eager to find more uses for their bumper crop, so they reached out to HydroGen, the largest green hydrogen firm in the world.

The company sent a letter to the Gang and the kids congratulating them for their creative thinking.

"Regrettably," the company wrote, "your Frog Frolic Reserve can't grow enough algae to make a difference in fuel research or production.

"But please, keep up the good work. Algae might be the most important living helper to humans in our future. Send us any new ideas you come up with. We'll be glad to give you credit. Who knows what we together will create."

Inspired by the letter and undaunted by the rejection, the kids were encouraged by Mrs. Hetzel's faith in them. The team pressed on with their work on clean fuels.

Led by Kwan, the son of the frog farm's former sluice manager and volunteer head of the Sluicers, witty kids brainstormed a hundred names for their group. They chose one to show they'd heard a message in the frogs' silence, and they planned to act on it.

The young rhymers claimed since "science" rhymes with "silence" people would know what they were all about. Few stretched their minds to the degree the young poets did, but everyone liked the name. They called their team the "Science of Frogs," or SOF.

"Hey, SOF sounds like SOS. *Science of Frogs, Silence in the Bogs*," a kid rhymed.

Another of the group, a former LFAer who'd just returned from basic training in the Army's Special Operations Forces, came up with another meaning for their acronym.

She said they were on a mission like no other. She told the group they were "Spec Ops for Frogs - Special Operations for Frogs."

The kids cheered her and adopted the "Spec Ops" name. SOF submitted algae research to the state's Young Scientists contest, winning second prize. Their efforts inspired the SOF to believe the frog Farm could reinvent itself as a fuel oil manufacturer or a carbon capture company.

"Maybe in the kids' lifetime," said coffee shop regulars. "God bless 'em for trying."

With more brainstorming, SOF came up with the idea of drying the algae and stuffing capsules with it to sell to vegetarians who needed Omega 3s.

"It's off topic but ...," Daria apologized. She was the most dedicated herbologist in the SOF. "Did you know Japanese people use knotweed to cure Lyme disease? It's supposed keep people young and limber."

"Amazing," Jess said. "Do they eat it?"

"They make tinctures!"

"We got so much knotweed we could supply every health food store in the country," David said.

"Promising ideas, folks" Mrs. Hetzel said. "Let's keep doing research before we jump into anything."

The SOF had so many ideas they formed a research posse, composed of four kids and Mrs. Hetzel, to prioritize their ideas. The most popular was to explore the potential of algae breaking down microplastics into their molecules.

Jess, one the most enthusiastic SOFers said, "That's the biggest problem in the world."

"That'n carbon in the air," said Daria.

Town vernal poolers got excited about their own research. They sorted themselves into teams, some raising tadpoles to be jumping frogs, some for meat, some for color and pets, and some for the songs and barks and croaks and trills they never lost faith in reviving.

Children of those dedicated vernal poolers eventually found themselves at the University biology department focused on reviving the frog song research by using cellular fermentation techniques.

In time, their research laid the groundwork for an almost miraculous project. By the time they graduated from college, the students had learned they could never monetize their education in the tiny frog meat and leather industry. Still, some of the most determined planned to disrupt the cattle and hog industry by applying cellular fermentation to produce modern bio-foods.

"Anyone who's eaten as much frog as I have will have no problem making cellular meat. In fact, I can't think of anything better to do with the IQ I inherited," said Neema, the high school's valedictorian.

She would become a *summa cum laude* graduate of her university's Food Science Department. Incorporating her frog research into designs for permaculture gardens with frogs for cityscapes, she won a national award from the Civic Revival Association out of Chicago.

Members of the first SOF research posse entered the University pledging to deepen their studies of algae. In response to their enthusiasm, the chemistry department and the biology department teamed up with three major companies. The grants funded studies in algae oil and micro-plastic conversions. The team found a partner in an enzyme developer to explore synergies in their research.

"It's a long-term investment," the ever-optimistic University president said when he announced the new program.

"Have you heard about algae power?" he said. "It makes fuel for trucks and cars. It absorbs carbon dioxide from the air. It can convert almost anything to almost anything. It feeds fish and frogs. It feeds people! Just think of all the roads and buildings the world needs to repair and build. Algae can make cement with no fossil fuels. Plankton Power to the People!"

Queen of the Wetlands

In honor of her saving jobs in the town with her restaurant, and for convincing James to donate the Frog Frolic Farm to the town, local businesses planned to erect a statue honoring Calli at the Reserve.

They needed an icon to feature on the town's website and its publicity materials. The businesspeople had learned their social media lesson so they didn't want to use mockable frog images or boring photos of cattails and cypress trees.

SOF and others protested because *Chez Calliope* had almost destroyed the frog farm, launching another generational conflict. Logic, insults, statistics, articles flew back and forth on social media and in the town's website and e-news site. Lawn sign and Twitter combat broke out.

"Don't make a monument to a criminal!"

"Smart minds know what's right."

"Don't trample on frogs' rights!"

"She did good for us!"

"We deserve a statue."

"She kept the town alive!"

"More tourists, less frogs!"

"More frogs, less tourists!"

"Art makes our town beautiful!"

"Statues can't sing like a frog."

"Calli gave us the Reserve!"

"Celebrate!"

The moderator of a local church, trained in managing difficult conversations, suggested a bridge to a solution: Listening to each other.

After months of citizen meetings, with the town council on the verge of calling a vote that could ignite a long expensive legal battle with the SOF and others, townspeople started to listen to each other.

The moderator's summary of the people's thoughts and feelings made sense to everyone.

"Calli was an entrepreneur whose business helped a lot of people survive even though the restaurant did much damage. But now look where she is. She reformed. Thanks to her vision and donations. The Reserve is a paradise!"

"She's no saint."

"Yeah! Don't forget the flies and the bird shit everywhere!"

"We never had so many good ideas in this town!"

"Are we better now than we were before?"

The activists and non-activists interested in the Reserve's future decided to take a vote on a proposal: An alliance of business owners, town councilors, random volunteers, and SOF members would design and name the memorial.

Community-minded Rosa persuaded the SOF to agree, but only if it was not named for the woman herself.

After more contentious talks, the alliance came up with a design and a name. They chose a local artist to sculpt a whimsical statue. It would be made of shiny copper and named Queen of the Wetlands. She would be decked out in full chef array.

The statue would face the ponds and the descendants of the frogs that had made her rich and whose silence created their own return to wild freedom.

A frog perched on top of her toque with one of its feet laid across its lips like a finger signaling silence. A warty toad peeked out of her apron pocket while a necklace of newts and salamanders circled her throat. The statue's face was peaceful and lit with smiles.

Some high school kids downloaded a symphony of frog calls and recorded it. Beside the statue, they installed an infinity loop of the music that played at the press of a button.

The popular choir of burps and peeps and chirps and grunts and barks at first thrilled then comforted the locals. Eventually, nostalgia for the lost world of random frog cacophony made the townsfolk sad. They stopped listening.

Tourists or school kids on a trip to the Reserve sometimes pressed the button, hearing frog rhythms and melodies, and marveling at the frog divas and divos dominating the chorus. When moisture shorted the speakers for the fifth time, nobody in town had the heart to replace them.

Butterflies of all hues, dragonflies, and every kind of flying frog food – gnats, midges, mosquitoes, flies, and no-see-ums – made the swamp their carefree year-round habitat.

Schools of small fish expanded making the Reserve a magnet to kids.

Reserve fishing policy allowed kids of any age to keep any fish they caught that was eight inches or longer. This was the strategy they expected would limit the growing bluegill, catfish, and largemouth bass populations.

As the frog and general amphibian population grew, egrets, herons, kingfishers, fly catchers and countless other swamp birds, bitterns, coots, mergansers, and mallards moved into the marsh world and stayed.

Hawks patrolled the skies above the ponds, thrilling hikers when they heard a red tail whistle.

Canada geese seemed to take detours over the swamps when they veed by in the fall and spring, honking and barking to each other. In the spring, the Reserve allowed a few geese couples to hatch eggs.

When the goslings could fly, all the geese were chased off the ponds. Nobody appreciated stepping on goose droppings on the trails.

Despite an influx of insatiable birds and preying land animals and their competition with voracious snapping turtles for fingerlings and flies, clever frogs of all species not only survived, sly tadpole by sly tadpole, their population expanded to its pre-Silence peak.

The frogs continued their quiet lives, lassoing insects with their tongues, hopping from mud humps to downed logs, diving and hiding from beaks and claws.

An unexpected and pleasing turn of events at the Reserve was the absence of mosquitoes and gnats and noseeums.

In the old days, when the Farm was in operation with non-stop, up-close frog racket, and daily frog harvesting, farmers often had to wear personal protective gear. On

100-plus degree, 90 percent humidity, days, farmers armored their bodies with facemasks and oxygen tanks to protect themselves from throngs of stinging bugs.

Hikers and walkers were appreciative of the Reserve's bugless conditions while the old timers knew there had to be a connection between the forsaking of frog farming and the now wild and free tadpoles' knack for feasting on mosquito eggs.

When out of town visitors approached the trail around the Reserve, they were puzzled by the sign posted at the head of the trail.

Do not spear
Do not spanghew
Do not gig
Do not harm frogs
Ever!

Kids under 10
can use bullfrogs for bait

Docents loved to explain the meaning of "spanghew."

The population of the box, snapping, and painted turtles ballooned. Since Calli and James had retired and moved away, only the oldtimers mentioned turtle soup or a pet turtle enterprise to promote the town.

On weekends, parents trekked down the grassy trails around the ponds with their children to watch the surface of the water for peering frog eyes. They listened as the frogs made delicate plinks and wavelets when they sensed the vibrations of footsteps or loud voices and dove to safety. Children spotted frogs darting their tongues to capture its lunch.

With so many butterflies swooping and darting and feeding the frogs, on one of his regular strolls, Mr. Clemens spotted a famed Amazonian butterfly. Its species was reputed to sip tears from the eyes of turtles. Inspired, he added a new Biology course in Lepidoptery, challenging his students to capture photo images, rather than catching and killing and mounting the delicate creatures.

"Ah, Mr. Clemens. That's no fun," boys would say.

"Here's why," Mr. Clemens said. "Butterflies in photos have vitality. They're much prettier than dry bugs pinned to a card. Besides, in ancient Greece, the word for butterfly also means soul. So why would you tack a beautiful soul up on your wall?"

As part of the creation of the town's new Reserve culture, citizens raised money to refurbish and expand the dilapidated frog museum. The LFA held a "Name the Museum" contest for everyone in the town. The overwhelming majority voted for the "Mr. Clemens Ranidae House."

One of the most popular exhibits was in the tropical greenhouse that was populated with frogs from equatorial forests and swamps around the world.

Strange frogs astonished the visitors. The "Fruititarian Frog" that drank the nectar of the milk fruit trees, the beautiful and fatal "Poison Dart Frogs," the transparent "Glass Frogs," the "Hairy Frogs," the cute "Desert Rain Frogs," and the "Flying Frogs" and other odd species.

The "Clemens House" became a must-visit place for biologists and herpetologists from all over the nation.

Rafts of playful otters moved into the Reserve. A beaver family felled trees that listed over the water. They thrived by munching the floating wild gardens of lily pads, entertaining human observers. Their industry raised the water level and deepened the swamps upstream.

The shoreline became home to clusters of newts with bright orange and yellow speckled skins glinting like daytime fireflies. In the sunset, the ponds shone fluorescent pink and orange, making the Reserve even more magical. Nighttime fireflies by the millions dazzled visitors on mid-summer evenings.

Often on summer nights, families would tiptoe along the shores with infrared flashlights so they wouldn't alert the frogs. Small blue lights from bioluminescent newts and frogs flickered like will-o-wisps around the ponds.

Docents counted whippoorwill songs to pass their time between moonlight tours of the ponds. The meteorologists among them devised a new system for predicting weather changes from the calls.

The system proved less accurate than frog calls, the weatherpeople admitted. Still, they posted their daily numbers on the Reserve's website just in case some predictable patterns would emerge.

Some youngsters reported sightings of a strange nighttime radiance in the woods, starting rumors of fairies and elves and ghosts. When a Reserve docent hiked into the forest edge, she discovered the source of the glow – foxfire, a fungus feasting on rotting wood. Despite the find, legends of magical creatures remained one of the charms of the Reserve.

The four-footed predator populace expanded apace with the frogs and their other prey. Once they'd reduced the errant frog amphibian population in the Remotes, they attacked the ponds' edges.

The Reserve reactivated the Farm's electric fences, not to keep frogs inside, but to fend off furry frog feeders. Daytime flying and swimming carnivores weren't affected, because during their evolution, the frogs had developed the acute vision and hearing needed to avoid most birds and clever large fish.

Still, herons pecked away at weeds and seeds and the occasional crawdad coasting by while herons sliced down into the muddy water to feed on small fish and heedless tadpoles.

Over time, people forgot about the frogs' constant chorus in the days before the Reserve. Instead, birds and insects and the occasional canine replaced the frog calls.

Sweet bird song in the mornings, other avian melodies throughout the day, owl hoots in the evening, cicadas and crickets well into the night, and random coyote howls satisfied the locals ears and longing for the wilds. Whippoorwill lamentations colored the nights with mystery.

Once in a while, a late walker would stop, look up and around, say to a companion, "Listen."

A lonesome croak or a short run of tree frog trills sharpened listeners' ears. They closed their eyes, focusing all their senses on sound. Rarely did the call repeat itself. If a ribbit or a croak lasted more than a few minutes, the news spread about that specific place on the trail. For the next few days, pond walkers would stop there, listen hard, then hearing only birds and insects, shake their heads and move on.

Over time, the copper sheen on the Queen of the Wetlands statue oxidized and morphed through moody, mossy colors until it settled into a soft green hue reminding some of the Statue of Liberty.

Today, the statue has sunk to its knees in the soft soil and tilts toward the water, bowing to the ancient amphibian world of mud and water and cypress and lily pads and cattails.

The Queen watches over the ponds and their legions of winged and finned predators and the bales of turtles and the knots of toads and the herds of landlubbing newts and the congresses of salamanders and the schools of fish, all in harmony with the silent frogs.

The XA

Improving animal feed or even coming up with new applications for algae felt to the SOF research team like meager efforts.

The group was stocked with imaginative kids with high energy and inexhaustable curiosity. They were eager to do something to make a radical change.

Musical SOFers composed an album of a frog symphony harmonizing frog calls from every continent. It was downloaded millions of times.

The SOF graphic arts team spun off a division to create video games and comics. Then, in concert with the musicians, they produced an animated film promoting the sights and sounds of the frog world, including calls that no longer pealed from the Reserve. The film, *Swamp Chorale*, became one of the 200 top YouTube videos of the month.

The budding teachers and graphic artists crafted a virtual reality experience of a tour of the Reserve, listening to the silence, and even scooping algae and frogs. They developed digital frog science shows designed for schools, universities, and museums around the world.

While the eager environmentalist artists popularized the *Swamp Chorale*, SOF kids formed a company to dive into possible inventions using frog parts, then to see if they could build an enterprise.

Lakshmi, one of the team's most diligent researchers, suggested they look into opportunities in the medical field.

"There's a lotta old people out there," she said. "My dad sells drugs to pharmacies. He said money from everywhere wants to get into medicine. 'Medical devices,' he told me."

"That's weird," Rosa said. "How does money want to get into pills and stuff?"

"I think it means people think medical stuff is a good business," Lakshmi said.

After sifting through online research papers with help from their genies, the downhearted team reported to Mr. Clemens the existence of the "Xenobot," a nano-medical gadget made with frog parts.

The Xenobot scientists had stumbled onto a "living machine" made from silicon and frog cells. They'd raised more than a million dollars to fund the design of the device.

It would carry medicines targeted to stubborn, metastatic cancer cells.

The SOF research group envied the idea.

"Wish we'd come up with that."

"None of our genies could come up with anything we havent already tried."

"That's that."

"Now what are we gonna do?"

"Hold on," Mr. Clemens said. "We could learn something from them. They have a brilliant idea. You're on the right track. I have faith you can build on their work or make something different. Much much better."

The SOF team sighed. Mr. Clemens was always a cheerleader, a fabulous teacher, but he didn't really know the crazy work research required. Some of the kids wanted to bail and have a good time, not spend all their lives in the lab deep diving into science that was already above their heads.

So, they hung out at each other's houses, listened to music, played video games, ate pizza, waiting around for somebody to come up with a brilliant idea that might not take too much work.

After observing their lassitude for a week, Mr. Clemens invited the team to his home for a barbecue.

"No wiggly frog legs," he promised.

Everyone showed up.

While they enjoyed a vegetarian barbecue with smoked frogs legs on the side, he said, "Look, it's the way of science. We need to get our momentum back. Remember what I told you about us scientists? We're all standing on the shoulders of geniuses – all hard workers."

"I'm standing on Shrek," Jeremy said.

"Look at me," Wei Min said, stretching his arms and leaning back and forth as if he was falling off a balance bar. "I'm standing on Paul Bunyan's head."

"Who's that?" Jeremy said.

Wei shrugged. "Some tall guy from Canada who chopped down giant trees by himself, with an ax."

The team turned to Mr. Clemens.

"He was a legendary woodsman in Minnesota, taller

than a two-hundred-year-old pine. He had a blue ox named Babe."

Wei grinned. "I like it up there in the clouds."

"At last, you admit your brain is like cotton candy, Wei," Jeremy said.

"Hey," Wei replied. "Clouds are dense, a big one can hold a billion pounds of water."

Lakshmi, ever polite, stood up.

"Get off Paul Bunyan's shoulders," she said. "He's the symbol of human predation on the planet. Invade, chop, clear, kill."

No one responded. Lakshmi stared at Wei while the group sat quietly.

Mr. Clemens clapped his hands.

"Let's move on. This is serious work. We have to do what we can. Study that Xenobot. It's just a stupid android run by a dumb AI. It's a first step but it's got a big weakness. It depends on silicon and electric power. We can do better.

"Let's have some fun with research. The first one who has a good research idea might get a free Einstein hoodie. From me."

The kids groaned. He'd given the entire team Einstein hoodies last Christmas.

"How about throwing us a taco party," someone said.

"That sounds fun," Mr. Clemens said. "Anybody needs an Einstein hoodie, let me know. I still have a bunch of green ones."

They decided to make a game of the research, organizing themselves into teams. The teams studied the Xenobot technology from as many angles as they could imagine.

Finally, they agreed the Xenobot was interesting but limited due to its silicon base structure. The Xenobot would have to compete with computers and cell phones and refrigerators and cars and every government, and every kind of "smart" device there would ever be for a supply of silicon.

"Making 'living' machines using gene-splicing is so old school. Machines age and break," Wei stated. "We want to help life evolve. Like my grandpa said just before he died, 'Life goes on.'"

"Who wants a machine made with plastics crawling around in their guts," Lakshmi said. "If it breaks and gets stuck, it'd kill you."

Within three months of learning about the "living machine," the hard-working SOFers proposed a concept that would lead to a radical and world-changing invention: An organic, healing creature made of the cells of frogs, not a machine.

The team reached out to physicist classmates to join the cause. They pooled scholarship funds to support the best business developers in the group to find money to fund their research.

Their main financial barrier was the funding for the enormous computer power they needed to conduct theoretical trials.

The business developers raised two million dollars from social media networking and crowdfunding by offering 1% of the company that would take the research to practical trials.

With widespread support mostly from peers, the SOF team won a ten million dollar grant from a pharmaceutical corporation.

The SOF team would experiment with the stem, skin, brain, and heart cells from the embryos of the African clawed frog (*Xenopus Laevis*) and the Panamanian golden frog (*Atelopus Zeteki*).

They attracted a few young National Institutes of Health researchers to help in the evenings. Using their access to state-of-the-art testing equipment and platforms, and after hundreds of secret physical experiments and thousands of digital test runs, the SOF team birthed their micro-cellular creature in digital form. Using the two main frog species' names, they called their undertaking the *XA Project*.

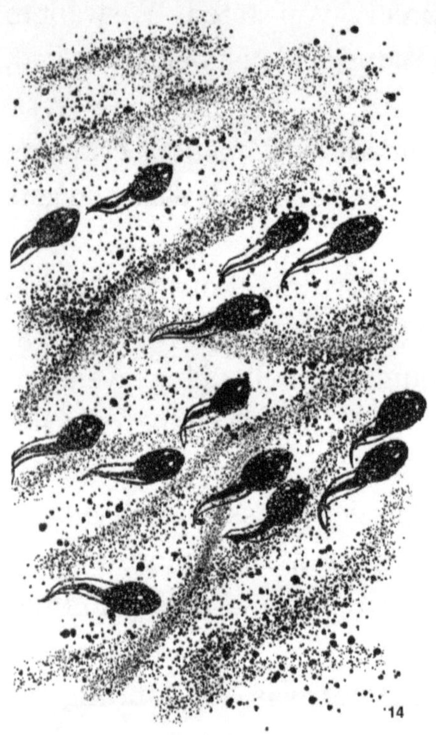

Practical entrepreneurs, they were mindful of the need to create and protect algorithms and formulas that would be nearly impossible to duplicate. They mixed into XA molecules parts from the Reserve's silent frogs with croaking American bullfrogs and the native wood frogs and amphibian species, and other common but secret materials.

They enlisted champion hackers to create and upgrade tricky, complicated cybersecurity systems to assure continuous unhackability for their work.

The next stage was to transform the digital work to organic matter and nano-cells. Smaller than a human blood cell and so resilient and adaptable, they could heal themselves from damage and survive for weeks.

As the shape of the XA evolved to its final form, the researchers observed it through the 3-D digital cell microscope. They chuckled when they saw the cells looked like wiggling tadpoles.

"Once a frog, always a frog," they joked.

Determined to revolutionize the nano-medical-robotics field, the team designed XA to be disguised as white blood cells so the body wouldn't reject them. They programmed the XA to deliver, collect, and destroy diseased cells and, when needed, to deliver medicine.

"Hey, Mr. Clemens," they texted him one morning, "we're going surfing!"

"What?"

"On galvanic waves! Ha!" The team had discovered that specific galvanic waves in cells caused particular illnesses. By following the galvanic waves, XA could collect and eradicate viruses, poisonous bacteria, cancer cells, malformed DNA or RNA.

The researchers aimed to solve what they surmised was the real cause of frog silence: plastics and other micro-pollutants. They focused on finding ways for XA to gather and absorb micro-plastics and other pollutants stored in adipose tissue or muscles or floating in body liquids.

The team worked with visionary chemists to invent a way of breaking down the components of the diseased and damaged cells and pollutants into their component molecules. They stored the molecules as gases in vacuum chambers. Some would be further disintegrated by enzymes then reassembled into products. Others would be turned into fuel.

Like a potent drug, an overdose of XA could cause disastrous stress on a person's metabolism. The team had formed the Devil's Advocates, the DevAds, an all-powerful squad of harsh critics dedicated to disprove, scorn, bash and trash any enthusiasms and unproved conclusions.

In their weekly "Thrash and Slam" meeting with the research team leaders, the DevAds refused to endorse the XA until somebody found a way to solve the biggest problem with the creature.

"Way ahead of you. We're halfway there," Jeremy, a grad student, countered. "Don't sweat it.

Ignoring him, the DevAds went on. "How do you fish them out of the body when they're done? Full of plastics, bacteria, viruses, dead cells?"

Wei Min stood up. "We'll gig 'em out!"

Some laughed, others frowned, recalling how, as little kids, they caught small Reserve frogs, stuck hooks into their brains and used them as bait to catch fish.

Mr. Clemens, who saw that the kids knew more, were smarter, and had the inner fire that his age had dampened some, cherished his role as cheerleader. He offered his guidance and encouragement whenever the kids' (of all ages) spirits flagged.

The team spent their big pharma grant and months of research to determine how to remove the used creatures from the body.

The body's powerful elimination organs solved the problem for them. Used-up XA passed through liver, the kidneys, the lungs, and the skin without damage to any organs or tissue.

When asked why XA could slip through the body even when chock full of toxins and debris, the team answered, "We don't really know. We guess because XA is all frog and organic matter. We'll work on it."

Discovering how to discharge the XA led them to the minimum effective dosage, the last critical problem to solve.

The team's caution slowed its introduction into the world but paid off in patient security.

Enthralled with their invention, none of the scientists had wondered if people would accept the treatment.

"Two thumbs up! They will," the team said when the DevAds raised the issue. "It's like bacteria. People inhale bacteria, viruses, dust, molds, all kinds of stuff with every breath. The XA is delivered by a shot. People are used to vaccinations."

"We've got proof they heal people. It's real. We had successful trials."

"Anybody can look at our evidence."

Mr. Clemens shrugged. "I believe in your work. It's sound, evidence-based, double bind tested. No serious negative reactions. But it's only a small sample. Now we wait to learn what the FDA and the real world say."

Existential risks

During their research, the team discovered a robust side effect they hoped would solve grievous health issues.

While the XA couldn't defeat every disease or mutation by direct attack, it amplified and strengthened the human immune system in cases of malaria, tuberculosis, corona viruses, bronchial issues, and a variety of other infections.

XA didn't heal or even treat all diseases, behavioral illness, or physical damage. The team warned, "If people don't take care of themselves, XA can't be their mothers."

As the design of XA progressed, the research team stumbled on a technique to produce XA from existing cells. They grew and froze billions of them, eliminating the need to ever use live frog cells again. It was almost as if they'd found a way for XA to reproduce.

"This has been the hardest work in my life," Angela, a team member said. "It's like the XA told us what to do next. We'd do one thing with it, then follow its lead to the next thing."

The tireless DevAds, confident they were the team's final

checkpoint before success or disaster and ever happy to criticize the ideas and the research, noted the latest obstacle with their customary sarcasm.

"If we may point out," they said in their mock-polite tone. "How will you stop XA from replicating out of control? The body knows how to make cancer cells. Why won't the immune system or some genius cancer cells control XA and metastasize it until all your flesh and bones are XAs?"

The team buckled down. They would insert a trigger to reverse the XA's assembly process when it reached 80% saturation with its target disease or toxins.

Still, with what Mr. Clemens called "a scootch of innocence," excited team members assumed, once they released XA, global appreciation would protect their invention from ill use.

"Don't be naïve and forget about the bad guys," Mr. Clemens said. "XA will attract the most destructive minds out there, for the challenge and their profit. No doubt there will be big money in it if they destroy or repurpose XA."

"Like what?" Jeremy, a promising intern said.

"Oh, I don't know," Mr. Clemens said to the group. "Think about it."

"They could infect XA with a mind control substance?"

"Yeah. Make people their slaves."

"Poison. Infect people then hold them hostage for billions of dollars."

"Colonize people's organs."

"Now you're starting to get it," Mr. Clemens said.

"Like make people's hearts burst."

"Take over governments."

"Adjust it somehow, insert it into dogs so they revert to their wolf natures."

"Wolf packs attack everyone!"

"Release it into the oceans with some kind of poisonous targeting thing."

"Yeah, an idea like that for cleaner fish. More fish maybe."

"Right. Clean up plastics infestation of the seas."

"Hold on. You're losing focus." Mr. Clemens said. "You don't have any idea about the risks criminals and the power-hungry would take advantage of."

Chagrined, several of the team shook their heads.

They called a meeting for the next day to consider the evils XA couldn't stop.

Mr. Clemens sat in, staying quiet while the team worked through the possibilities.

"We can't release XA. It's too dangerous. Someone could use it to destroy civilization."

"Every brilliant thing has a dark side," Imeela said, hopelessness tinging her words. "It's too much of a risk."

"An existential risk."

"What's that?"

"Something that destroys civilization, like a meteor strike."

"Like a pandemic, only worse."

Imeela noted, "Every day's an existential risk in this world."

Nobody moved for a minute until she said, "We have to do something or we can forget about XA forever."

"Delete, burn all our research so nobody can ever use it."

"Too sad."

"Goddam it."

To a person, the team groaned. "What do we do?"

Mr. Clemens said, "Take a break. Walk around. Have some lunch. Then, go back to the drawing board."

"That could take months."

"Years."

"Does time matter for XA?" Mr. Clemens asked. The group went silent.

"You can do it," Mr. Clemens smiled. Then, he clapped his hands like the schoolteacher he was. He reached into his pocket, extracting three hacky sacks, started juggling them.

The researchers wondered what he was trying to tell them. "We need to open our minds to the criminal mind," the team leader said. "What kind of attackers do we defend against? People? Weapons?"

The group's team mind exploded with evil ideas, filling the room like steam boiling off a sweet corn pot.

"A mutating agent."

"Like it turns XA into alien beacons and the earth gets invaded."

A few laughed.

"A bio-remora that clings to XA and spits out toxins it already thought it cleaned up."

"Mech."

"Virus."

"A virus that absorbs XA's powers and makes it destroy itself."

"A sleeper that lingers in the patient until XA has done its work. Then it does something terrible to the patient."

"O my god."

"A million times."

One of the most thoughtful and respected members raised her hand. "These are good bad ideas, but what if someone wants to do even more good than we can imagine?"

"They come to us. That's all," the leader said. "XA can't do everything. Remember, once XA goes global – you know it will – the feedback will keep us busy updating and adjusting. We gotta keep it as simple as we can."

"All right. I like that," the most respected member said. After a moment, she added, "Here's what I think we should do. Any attempt to even touch XA by anything it's not programmed to identify will cause it to stop working immediately."

An electric charge flowed through the group.

"If something goes after it, XA will go still. Then it dissolves into its molecules and makes a quick exit from the body. Our cybersecurity won't be beat ... we hope ...."

"That's it. We can do that."

"Nothing's perfect."

"How about this. If something gets clasped up with XA inside somebody, there's some way to shut it off."

The team liked the idea but nobody liked slowing progress even more.

"Time to go back to work," Mr. Clemens said.

So they did. After nine months of inspired theory, lab-controlled experiments, and careful field work with volunteers, XA was ready to protect and defend itself. It had no armor. Its defense was its sensitivity to unwanted touch and an immediate, nimble disappearance from the body.

They kept this final discovery under wraps until they

were ready to bring the XA to the wide world.

Mr. Clemens told the SOF team that they might have invented what some might consider a new species. "Since XA replicates, some media will go crazy on it, call it a new domain of life."

The team looked at each other, smiling and pumping fists. "But, don't believe them," Mr. Clemens said. "You've reconceived and reorganized. The creation is in your bodies and minds. Think about that."

"*Yo, Mr. Clemens.*"

He went on. "You put more than your mental power into it. You made XA your hearts and souls."

Some of the kids cracked up, others put their hands together as in prayer and bowed their heads.

Always enjoying repartee with Mr. Clemens, Wei said, "Is XA a new religion?"

Lakshmi looked at him. "Be respectful."

"I am," Wei retorted. "Mr. Clemens is our high priest!"

Mr. Clemens said, "That's cute, Wei. But it's not a religion.

"And we don't have priests or monks or nuns. We have you and I don't see a holy person in the room. Except you, Imeela, with those holey jeans you wear."

The room exploded with relieved laughs. Imeela chuckled, not one bit embarrassed.

"When people are healed," Mr. Clemens continued. "You can celebrate your hard work. You are sort of like parents, now. Let's be grateful for XA, your brainchild. Now what's your most important next step?"

He paused as the group waited for a joke.

"Take care of it," Mr. Clemens said.

SOF had numerous colleagues in the global biotech research community who had worked in companies based on radical biotech innovations. While the FDA pored over the XA records, SOF contacted a few trusted venture capital funds and friendly wealthy families. They all vied to invest whatever dollars, euros, yen, pounds, francs, or renminbi were needed to complete testing and into the market.

With a keen eye on the planet's growing populations and migrations, the founders chose confidential investors from every continent with an emphasis on African and Indian and South American firms. The investors had to prove their honesty, commitment to human rights, and planetary health.

At no time were the savvy SOF founders tempted to give up the least control of their work to any moneyed interest.

The SOF laid out three conditions for financing.

First, the venture capitalists would fund all the research it would take to bring frog song back to the Frog Frolic Reserve, if the town still wanted that.

Second, necessary funds would go to research and develop global distribution to health practitioners via a satellite-based platform. The app would make treatments available at a cost anyone could afford.

Third, the financiers would fund the frog town's school science, literature, humanities, and music programs for the next hundred years.

The FDA approval came quickly for small doses and treatments of specific diseases. Selected patients worldwide who were injected with XA became well with no major side effects or abject failures.

Some SOF researchers were so obsessed with the possibilities of the XA they dropped out of school to concentrate full-time on the project. Those who had jobs, quit them and devoted themselves to their work on the deepest, most intoxicating possibilities they could imagine.

Their dedication paid off. XA would be available worldwide via *Médecins San Frontiers* and non-profit health care organizations, for medical help for billions of people without health care. They knew they'd discovered something life-changing for the world.

Simultaneously, their hacker team raised XA cybersecurity levels equal to or, the team insisted, beyond the Department of Defense systems. Their intercontinental cybersecurity team was as good as any anywhere in the world.

Kyara, one of the chief graphic designers, contacted James, who was living with Calli and raising oyster and shiitake mushrooms a few miles from the Reserve. She asked him if the SOF could use the Frog Frolic Farm's *Singing Frog* logo for their work. James said he'd be honored and so would the frogs.

"We'll keep your basic idea," Kyara said. "We have to change it, bring it up to date."

"Do whatever you want," James said.

From t-shirts and caps to exotic frog patterned fabric and coats and any imaginable object, the Silent Frog logo became a global symbol for health, creativity, and environmental well-being.

Rosa was in the tenth grade, thrilled to be an SOF

assistant researcher when they invented the XA. When she and her friends wore their Singing Frog hoodies around town, she felt happy, hoping one of the benefits of the XA would be that the frogs would sing like in the old days.

If not, maybe she could make that happen. Her mind had been at work for years on the challenge. Gene-splice a working frog larynx? CRISPR some frog eggs that grew into croakers and peepers? Design an additive to water to activate frog song?

Rosa had a hundred ideas.

Rosa's dance

With the earnings from the XA Project, the SOF entrepreneurs established a foundation to support a global tournament for what they named the *S Prize* in honor of the frogs' inspiring silence.

They announced the prize worldwide and engaged a jury of eminent scientists for the S Prize Award Team. The S Prize competition was open to inventors or researchers from anywhere, the more outrageous the proposal, the better.

The call for submissions said, "It's all about life as we know it and life as we help it evolve. If you want to do something outrageous and beautiful, and have an original idea you can test, apply for the S Prize!"

The Research Director of the IT department at Tsinghua University joined the President of the Worldwide Future Foundation, the Brazilian Nobel Prize winner for gamma wave study, and the Chief Marketing Officer for Aqua Earth Society as the chief decision makers for the S Prize.

Aimed to stimulate biotech discoveries, the winners

would receive funds and connections with senior scientists and researchers to pursue whatever specialty they chose.

Rosa went online and submitted a one-page proposal to research her “Theory of Amphibian Telepathy.” Rosa’s idea for S Prize research was to study frog physiology with a focus on electromagnetic cardio impulses.

Her pitch aimed to show how her theory, when fully developed, would help humans. She also pointed out, salamanders and most toads and frogs didn’t croak or signal in any hearable way and their populations kept growing. Some of them could even regrow lost appendages and other parts.

When her grandmother heard about Rosa’s telepathy theory, she said, “Mi Rosamundo. Telepathy? Did you get that idea from me,” she raised her eyebrows innocently. “You know I practice telepathy every day.”

“You do?”

“It’s called prayer.”

“This is a little different, grandma,” Rosa said, raising her eyebrows, smiling and mimicking her grandmother.

“If you say so. Every day I telepath with many others – Ulphia, Maria – sometimes I get brave enough to telepath with Jesus.”

“That’s cool. Maybe frogs are praying to each other? Like sending out radar asking who will be my mate?”

“Rosa, it’s not funny. Prayer fixes a lot of things that are wrong. Not everything, but ... I always get an answer, even if I don’t like it.”

“I’m not trying to be funny, Grandma. It might be something like prayer, only between frogs, not saints and people.

"Not only that. They warn each other about fishes and foxes. I think they can tell each other where the best mud is. I have a theory. They can talk to other creatures, too. Like the weeds. Like how they sing to flies to attract their lunch and dinner."

"I'll pray for you, Preciosa."

Rosa hugged her grandma, saying, "Te amo, Abuela."

Directions for the contestants allowed them full use of any researched resources they could find – friends, families, teachers, any tech in any field.

The instructions read, "If your entry reaches the top one hundred, we'll audit your research trail. The top one hundred will show some mastery of the research process. We will judge your entry based on your vision, imagination, and the impact of your proposal.

Winners will be people with original ideas, not collectors and combiners of information. We expect to see your failure paths as well as your successes."

The S Prize site was inundated by emails with rough ideas about fantastic solutions to the most profound human and environmental problems. When the S Prize first level AI review team narrowed the ridiculous and false notions down to the merely preposterous but substantial, the SOF team felt sure, no matter who won, the contestants would change the world.

A fourteen-year-old physicist from Belgium promised he could deliver a provable theory of human immortality.

A political science teacher from Shanghai indicated she was on the brink of proving a way to change human behavior so empathy and creativity could be the default settings in the brain.

A virtual reality inventor from Lima showed a trailer of people walking, fully aware, with no headgear, onto a balcony on a skyscraper and rising over the railing, flying over the city then scooting over the Andes and Brazil far over the Pacific before diving to the bottom of the Mariana Trench.

A thirteen-year old chemist from Chile proposed to identify "forever chemicals" lodged or floating in organic matter. That would be the basis for her development of a system to capture and remove them. These ideas struck Rosa as miraculous. She was inspired by the team from Lagos who believed they'd invented a device that would allow 3D printing using any materials, even leaves and rocks, not just plastics.

The jury of senior scientific and legal advisors used the analytic and predictive power of its genie to winnow the global competition to one hundred finalists. The jury's diverse team also rated the quality of the contestants' ethical attitudes.

After video-interviewing all one hundred, and two months after she submitted her proposal, the Award Team chose seventeen-year-old Rosa to be one of the top ten applicants. The ten finalists now had to submit a proposal detailing how their work, if successful, would benefit the world and why they should receive an award. Not least, an outline of their plans for the prize money.

The finalists' abstracts were available for anyone to read.

Upon learning about her award, some of the other finalists objected. Rosa was too young and inexperienced. She won the go-ahead because she was a member of SOF and a favorite of the funders. She would never be able to handle the research work because she had no lab at her disposal.

Their main complaint was that her topic was stupid and useless. "Who Cares About Frog Talk?" headlined caustic posts and snarky posts from sore losers across nearly every media platform.

The SOF declared Rosa was an ideal Spec Ops Frog member, a leader and an inspiring bio-thinker. Besides, no SOFers participated in reviewing the proposals or deciding anything about who would be given a chance for the top prize.

"Get with it," they pronounced. "Young people are geniuses!"

Rosa felt terrible for the SOF. She felt she should withdraw her proposal until Mr. Clemens heard of her intention.

"Everybody outside our town makes fun of frogs," she said. "All over the internet. They think frogs are slimy and dumb."

"Don't doubt yourself or your work, Rosa." He was angry at her detractors. "Focus. Forget those jealous idiots complaining about your proposal. As we scientists might say, 'The world is made up of protons, electrons, and neutrons. We forgot about the morons.'"

"Right, Mr. Clemens," Rosa said, dubious.

He said, "You're doing important science. Good will come of it. You have what we call 'the scientist's instinct.' The nose for discovery. Your vision is the clearest I've ever seen in a student. Even among adult research scientists I know. You are a hunter! So get to work!"

Mr. Clemens, among his other gifts, was prescient.

After heart-wrenching talks with her parents and best friends, Rosa moved ahead to plan her research. Her social life, the little there was of it, her grades, her hair, her complexion, all suffered. Rosa noticed, but she didn't care. She was busy, immersed in her dream.

She was fascinated with the scientific method and cherished its principles: Get an idea, test it, fail, analyze what went wrong, gather more facts, update, test, fail, update, do it again and again. Then if you're lucky, formulate a theory to work with.

The most difficult thing she'd accepted about science research in general was, if your theory was good enough, other scientists must try to prove you wrong. She'd have to find irrefutable evidence of Amphibian Telepathy.

Ever since Rosa had first heard that most, but not all, frogs croaked and trilled and barked and peeped as part of their mating, she'd wondered why no one yet knew how silent frogs communicated.

When she was a child, Rosa's parents had taken her for frequent hikes around the Farm and the Reserve. She saw something new every time, feeling like a different person on every hike. Even as a ten-year old she knew, in her own animal sensitivity, that silent frogs could communicate with each other, even if people couldn't hear.

When she discussed the idea with her friends, parents, Mr. Clemens, and Henny her tutor, they agreed. Or seemed to.

Henny said in its clipped accent, "Whatever you need, Rosa."

"Maybe they talk with their eyes," fellow young scientists surmised.

"Some kind of chemical exchange?" Wei Min suggested. "Pheromones are a basic animal communication tool."

Violet joked, "We don't know, but I guess the frogs have it covered ... I mean *clasped*."

Rosa laughed.

She liked Wei Min's idea so she tested it first, then discarded it. Pheromones would disperse too easily in water and even if another frog sensed it, they'd never know exactly where it came from, foiling the intent of the sender's desire.

Early in The Silence, researchers had studied frogs' mouths with the bulging membranes' sound paths. They'd learned that frog croaks caused the membrane to vibrate and the inner ear to spark with electrical charge in male, female, and the rare hermaphrodite ("Both-Together-Now") frog.

Rosa thought about the fact that frogs had eardrums on the surface of their skin that were often larger than their eyes. She wondered if that had to do with other organs, too. Lungs, skin, even their hearts since their beats followed steady electrical pulses.

She loved her conversations about amphibian telepathy with Mr. Clemens as well as with the aging and still teaching Mrs. Hetzel. They helped Rosa think through her ideas and articulate them in writing and speaking.

During her junior year in high school she'd taken college level biology. By her senior year, about the time SOF announced the S Prize, Rosa's self-confidence in her scientific talent had blossomed.

When Rosa compared her own ideas with the other finalists, she decided she would have no chance to win, but she didn't care. She'd try anyway simply because she loved research and she felt frogs were some of the most beautiful animals on earth, including humans.

Most of all, she'd try because she loved her old pet frog Henny. She knew some people thought she was crazy because she loved that little thing as much, or more, than people loved their dogs and cats.

I'm a scientist because Henny inspired me, she thought. I'll do it for them and all the other wild creatures nobody cares about. And I'll do it for me.

Once she'd decided to compete for the S Prize and take the risk for the sake of pleasing herself, she asked Mr. Clemens to help her find the tools she'd need.

He called Ms. Subhoda, Dean of the University Science department, reminding her about all of the brilliant students his little town had supplied to the school over the years.

He discussed Rosa's extraordinary talents and drive. He said he could gather not only academic references, but countless character references supporting her. He emailed the Dean some of Rosa's high school papers, all filled with innovative ideas based on basic scientific research.

Mr. Clemens concluded his call saying, "You probably remember Einstein considered what he did was basic scientific research."

The Dean, thrilled to learn of Rosa's qualifications, immediately granted her permission to use the biology, chemistry, and digital tech labs and access their equipment and historical data, whatever she needed.

"Of course," the Dean Subhoda said. "I have to mention the cost of the university's computer time and maintenance of any equipment Rosa might need."

"Let me know how much it will be and we'll take care of it," Mr. Clemens volunteered.

When the expected costs arrived, Mr. Clemens took a deep breath and sat back. He had no idea modern lab research would be so costly. He called Rosa's dad to give him the bad news.

"No worries, Sam," her dad said. "We'll manage somehow. I believe in my daughter's dreams."

Within a few weeks, Rosa's parents and Mr. Clemens and some generous townspeople pooled their funds to pay for the university fees. One of her supporters, one of the wealthiest citizens in town, told Mr. Clemens, "We have no kids. Whatever she needs, we'll help."

Ms. Subhoda offered to give Rosa college credit for the work she did, if she submitted a report.

Rosa told her, "That's okay. I'll send you my S Prize work, but you don't have to give me college credit. I'd like it, but to be honest, I might go somewhere else for college. I should have applied already, but I haven't had time to think about it."

Rosa buckled down to study the brain images of frogs collected from dozens of species of voluble frogs and the several silent species of the Reserve and others from around the world. She aimed her studies at different kinds of animal sonar. Learning was play.

The university Biology department gave her access to BIO7.77, the most advanced and secure biology research AI available.

With 7.77, Rosa created a secure personal AI she named after her childhood pet frog, "Henny." She and Henny refined her searches and filed her sources and discoveries, failures and successes.

She learned that owls roosting in the tops of trees could hear a mouse's heart beating in the grasses below. Owls could hear the rumble of a possum's stomach while it was inside its den.

As she listened to whale song, she grasped the fact that most beings communicate in ways beyond human imagination.

"Whales use sonic and subsonic and supersonic messages," she thought. "Maybe grandma is on to something about prayers. Evolution has devised ways for organic beings to communicate telepathically."

Rosa knew trees communicate through fungi underground and in the air via chemical transfers from their leaves and needles. Her reflections led to a sci-fi insight that maybe rocks talk to each other in frequencies so low our most sensitive machines can't identify them.

Rarely attending her high school classes, Rosa hyper-focused on her research. She tested the notion of frog sonar, a subvocal sound wave that vibrated the water in particular ways.

Rosa "borrowed" dozens of frogs and gallons of water from the Reserve ponds. She immersed the frogs in a swamp-like setting in the lab to test the theory.

She used ultra-sensitive sonar equipment to listen for revealing tones and watched the monitors for traces of sonic waves. The machine picked up no sound waves other than water sloshing and unidentifiable notes and static.

Perhaps it was her keen eyes or lifelong intuition or Henny's research or luck, when one day she detected what might be a slight enlargement in Reserve frog brain cells just behind the camouflaged inner ear.

Feeling tentative, Rosa reported her finding to the lab chief. Impressed, he gave her access to the school's prize microscope.

Day after day, often into the solitary night, she examined diaphanous slice after slice of frog brain. The lab had never allowed her to enhance the microscope to its maximum power.

Rosa begged the lab chief to expand the light microscope to its maximum 2,000x magnification.

"Tell you what. You've proven you're a gifted researcher. Just this one time, I'll let you use our scanning electron microscope. It's not the best in the world, but you'll be happy," he said. "It cost more than a billionaire's mansion. I'll reserve if for tomorrow afternoon."

"O my god. This is the luckiest day of my life," she thought. To the professor, she said, "Don't worry. I'll be super careful. You can watch me."

"That won't be necessary. I'll be in my office if you need me."

The one day she now had permission to use the microscope was also the day of her high school's Spring Cotillion, so she would have to leave early enough to dress for the dance.

At first, Rosa couldn't understand the mysterious details the electron microscope revealed at its magnification of 1.5^4 x. After scanning blurry-eyed for an hour, she detected a nano-tangle of neurons tucked inside a female frog's inner ear.

By early afternoon, Rosa felt excited and distracted by her upcoming Cotillion but, ever the driven researcher, she decided to buckle down as long as she could.

When she peered at her screen showing the area where she'd noticed the nearly invisible bump, there it was, ten miles wide in front of her nose.

At that moment, her father arrived early to pick her up. "You're way early, Dad. I might be onto something. Get a cup of coffee or something. It's free in the lab kitchen. They have some bear claw pastries today, too."

When he reminded her about the dance, she said, "No worries. I don't have a date. I can get there whenever."

"You'll regret it if you miss your senior Cotillion."

"I know, I know. I'm going. Just not yet."

Rosa hadn't found enough evidence to back up her theory. She suggested that her father go home and come back in a couple of hours. He left, smiling, feeling proud of her.

She pored over the recorded images for two more hours, eventually identifying similar tangled auditory ossicles in females that might cancel ambient noise. Perhaps this was how they could listen only to their special boys' appeals.

Her dad returned.

"It's after dinner. We have to go."

"Almost. Pleeeese? It won't take me long to get ready."

He went into the kitchen to try another pastry.

Rosa placed male frog brains on the display plate. She laughed out loud when she found a miniscule node hidden between the male frogs' larynxes and their brain. When she stimulated the node with a tiny electric pulse, the larynxes vibrated at about 3,200 Hz, the same register as a normal bullfrog croak.

Rosa jumped up from her seat and screamed. "We did it! Henny! We did it!"

She had discovered how frogs communicated sub-vocally.

Her dad sprinted in from the next room.

"Rosamundo, what's going on? Are you alright?"

She hugged him. "I'm perfect, Dad. I couldn't be better. I found something cool."

He stared at her.

"I think it's the source of frog telepathy. I don't know how it works. That will be the next phase," she said.

Finally, half an hour, Rosa said, "Let's go, Dad. Either I have something or I don't. It's the best I can do."

They hurried home where Rosa changed into her new red dress and sped off to the Cotillion. She felt more elated than she'd ever been.

Known as someone who studied all the time and who was smarter than most teachers, Rosa shocked her classmates with exhilarated non-stop dancing and energetic singing and rapping.

"Rosa, I can't believe you," Violet said

"I'd like some of that drug," Wei chimed in.

"No, I don't do drugs. You know that. I'm just happy."

"Don't tell me. You fell in love," he said.

Rosa grinned, bouncing up and down on her toes and slinging her arms and shaking her booty in tune to the music.

"This is me," she told Wei. "I found how frogs talk with each other. They don't have to make a peep!"

"Holy shit!" Wei said, hugging her.

Her friends laughed and copied her wild dancing.

"Remember our frog dances when we were little kids?" Wei shouted. "Let's hop and leap and jump like crazy frogs!"

Rosa's exuberance and wild moves affected all the dancers.

The band said later the audience drove them to play out of their minds. Her class voted Rosa the Star of the Cotillion.

The next day, Rosa slept past noon. She still didn't know how her discoveries would help humans, but she was exhilarated about her finding.

She wrote up "A Theory of Frog Telepathy" and added a few sketches showing how it might function.

She admitted she didn't really understand how the electrical impulses crossed between frogs. She made a modest suggestion that the telepathy might happen in the undetectable quantum flux. That would require extensive research, or as she noted, "... swimming deeper and farther with frogs ...."

Rosa emailed her proposal to the S Prize committee.

Six weeks later, she received a text followed by a phone call telling her she'd won an S Prize. Her idea and her preliminary research won fifth prize.

She didn't believe it. She sat staring at her computer.

Fifteen minutes later, Mr. Clemens called. When she picked up she heard him shout, "You won! You won!"

For a second he sounded to Rosa like a bullfrog braying. Shivers rolled up and down her arms and back.

Always humble and polite to others, she said, "Thank you. Thank you. Thank you. I just read the text. If it weren't for you, Mr. Clemens, I'd still be dissecting frogs and stinking of formaldehyde. Wait till Doc hears about this!"

They laughed. Rosa invited him for a celebratory dinner and walk with her and her family at the Reserve after things settled down. Rosa couldn't stop smiling for days.

All the S Prize winners met over video and became best friends. The town erected billboards at its borders: "Home of Rosa, S Prize Winner" and published a video interview with her on the council's website.

The S Prize first place went to the woman from Shanghai who developed a theoretical collection of bacteria that, when triggered by a stream of up and down quarks and stirred into radioactive waste from nuclear medicine, power, weapons, and research, would reduce the half-life of the nuclear waste to less than a hundred years.

Second went to a kid who invented a solar cell built of recyclable, common materials that had tripled the sunlight conversion power of existing cells.

An inventor from Guam who designed a nanoskin exoskeleton, made from bamboo, hemp, mushrooms, and bovine bone that would cleave to and strengthen any physical body, needy or healthy, won third prize.

A bioengineering team that claimed to have found a gene that would allow humans to levitate and move across any terrain a foot above the ground, in certain weather conditions, won fourth prize.

The first four prizes were awarded for such stunning insights and inventions that Rosa was dumbfounded that her minor discovery won a prize.

The S Prize judges assured her that she won for her visionary work and opening a new direction in biomedical research of connectivity in brain networks.

In Rosa's acceptance video, she said, "I sent my research to my friends who love genetics.

"My good friends Wei and Violet love biotech. They're

starting a business to find if there are any common genetic reasons for the frogs' silence. If not, they may create some, or not.

"Who knows? Our silent frogs could ripple the waters of evolution. They could help everybody everywhere. Human and wild!"

Back on the Reserve

On the Frog Frolic Reserve, even as the nights warmed and many seasons endured heavy downpours with high winds and others brought droughts and random frosts, frogs thrived among abundant hues of flowering plants and algae and duckweed in a bee-hummed tranquility.

Cherishing the primal world of the Reserve, visitors followed the guidelines posted on hand-carved and painted signs at the entrance.

Picnic in Peace
No pets
No smoke
Slow strolling encouraged
Yay naps!

The docents, the Weedies, and the Sluicers made themselves available to answer questions about the ponds, updating the latest news of the plants' and animals' cycles of life and death.

People of all ages marveled at the beauty of the Reserve,

finding solace and inspiration in the humid swamplands. Some called the Reserve a temple, others their church. Many felt it was a shrine to ancient Earth.

Most of the year, birdsong seemed to rise out of the waters. Wrens and warblers piped silvery invitations, peewees jingled delicate lovesongs, hawks squealed what could be glee. Ducks quacking sounded like bull frogs barking.

Osprey and bald eagles swooped down to snatch naïve frogs and careless fish. Kingfishers and herons busied themselves on the shores, while crows, ravens, and buzzards shared abundant scavengings.

In the summer dusk, firefly extravaganzas lit the ponds and awed visitors ambling the trails.

Nights, the wetlands rustled with activity. Bats kited and swifts cruised through swarms of insects over the ponds. Owls hooted, foxes barked, coyote packs howled.

Autumn and winter evenings, listeners might hear the lonely cry of a visiting loon. Later, other than forlorn whoops of whippoorwills, the Reserve was a haven of silence.

Content to sit and feed in the humid air, follow their natures to make tadpoles, hop, swim, and bury themselves in swampy silt, perhaps listening to the tantalizing buzz of insects and the melodic ripples of water, the frogs kept their peace.

Day or night, no frogs croaked, chirped, or trilled. Not one ribbit was heard.

Not a gack. Not a gung. Not a peep.

Thank You

Thank you, Maureen Moore, my painter and writer friend, you helped me make this book. Your patience is incomparable and your good humor is a blessing. When I asked you how many drafts we'd done, you said, "I don't have enough fingers and toes to count them on!"

Thank you, Billie Timmins, you alerted me to how precious frogs are, especially the delicate little ones.

Thank you, Thomas Dudley, you grasped my vision for the book and portrayed it with your inimitable work.

Thank you, David Grant, for your sharp eye, keen ear and encouragement on so many projects we've worked on together over the years.

Thank you, Claude and Shirley, for showing me how optimism and resilience bring freedom, creativity, and happiness.

Also by Thomas Timmins

Novels
The Hour Between One and Two (Trilogy)
Blood Medicine
The Special Fruit Company
Down at the River
Aphrodisiac for an Angel
The Silence of Frogs

Short Fiction
Puff of Time
Visions of My Other Self
Desert Dusk Music
Don't Worry - The Safety's On
Ding Dong Cart

Graphic Verse Novel
Zom

Poetry
Likings for Shadows
I Was Just Laughing
Food Breaks Free
Almost Everyone
some say yes
Never Been Here Before
between worlds
card tricks
Questions?
3 little words

www.thomastimmins.com

www.ingramcontent.com/pod-product-compliance
Lightning Source LLC
Chambersburg PA
CBHW060805310726
48980CB00002B/239

* 9 7 9 8 9 9 2 7 1 5 4 4 6 *